Joyce
Marx
Defoe Abbott Hardy Machiavelli Montaigne Chesterton Cooper Emerson Austen
Melville Haggard Hugo
Eliot Grimm
Stoker Carroll Christie Molière
Wilde Byron Schiller
Maupassant Engels
Garnett Einstein Fitzgerald Hawthorne Kafka
Goethe Smith Hall
Cotton Dostoyevsky
Baum Kipling Doyle Willis
Henry Nietzsche
Leslie Dumas Flaubert Turgenev Balzac
Stockton Vatsyayana Crane
Burroughs Verne
Curtis Tocqueville Gogol Vinci
Homer Widger Tolstoy Whitman Busch
Darwin Thoreau
Potter Freud Twain Scott Plato Harte
Kant Zola Lawrence Dickens Burton Hesse
Jowett Stevenson
Andersen Cervantes
London Descartes Voltaire
Poe Aristotle Wells Cooke
Hale James Hastings Irving
Bunner Shakespeare
Richter Chambers
Doré Dante da Shaw Benedict Alcott
Swift Chekhov Pushkin
Wodehouse Newton

 tredition®

The Female Gamester

A Tragedy

Gorges Edmond Howard

Imprint

This book is part of TREDITION CLASSICS

Author: Gorges Edmond Howard
Cover design: Buchgut, Berlin – Germany

Publisher: tredition GmbH, Hamburg - Germany
ISBN: 978-3-8424-3203-1

www.tredition.com
www.tredition.de

THE FEMALE GAMESTER

A TRAGEDY

By Gorges Edmond Howard

Et quando uberior vitiorum copia? quando Major avaritiae patuit sinus? alea quando Hos animos? neq; enim loculis comitantibus itur, Ad casum tabulae, posita sed luditur arca. Juv. Sat. I. Sure none in crimes could erst beyond us go! None such a lust for sordid avarice show! Was e'er the Die so worn in ages past? Purses, nay Chests, are now stak'd on a cast.

To the Countess of Charlemont, the Lady Viscountess Southwell, and Lady Lifford.

As the example of Persons of rank and quality, must ever have a powerful influence upon all others in society, and as I know none among the many eminently virtuous characters of your sex, (for which this kingdom is above all others distinguished) with whom I have the honour of being acquainted, more conspicuous than your Ladyships, for excellence of conduct in every female department in life, I, therefore, thus presume in taking the liberty of presenting the following DRAMATIC ESSAY to your patronage, and am, with the highest respect,

Your Ladyships' Most obedient servant, &c. The Author.

Contents

To the Reader.

I have always been of the same opinion with the Author of the Preface to the translation of Brumoy's Greek Theatre; in which, speaking of Tragedy, he hath expressed himself in the following lines: "In England, the subject is frequently too much exalted, and the Scenes are too often laid too high. We deal almost solely in the fate of Kings and Princes, as if misfortunes were chiefly peculiar to the great. But our Poets might consider, that we feel not so intensely the sorrows of higher powers, as we feel the miseries of those who arc nearer upon a level with ourselves. The revolution and fall of empires affect us less, than the distresses of a private family. Homer himself had wandered like Ulysses, and although by the force of imagination he so nobly described the din of battle, and the echoing contests of fiery princes, yet his heart still sensibly felt the indigence of the wandering Ithacan, and the contemptuous treatment shewn to the beggar, whose soul and genius deserved a better fate."

This having confirmed me in my opinion, I set about the following dramatic attempt upon that horrid vice of Gaming, of all others the most pernicious to society, and growing every day more and more predominant amongst all ranks of people, so that even the examples of a Prince, and Princess, pious, virtuous, and every way excellent, as ever a people were blessed with, contrary to the well-known axiom,

> Regis ad exemplum totus componitur orbis, have had but small effect.

I finished it, part in prose, and part in blank verse, in about six weeks, and having shewn it to several of my literary acquaintance, the far greater part were of opinion, that it should be entirely one, or the other; but, as the scene was laid in private life, and chiefly among those of middling rank, it ought to be entirely prose; and that, not much exalted; and accordingly, with no small labour, I turned it all into prose. But in some short time after, having communicated this to Dr. Samuel Johnson, his words (as well as I remember) were, "That he could hardly consider a prose Tragedy as dramatic; that it was difficult for the Performers to speak it; that let it be either in the middling or in low life, it may, though in metre and spirited, be properly familiar and colloquial; that, many in the middling rank are not without erudition; that they have the feelings and sensations of nature, and every emotion in consequence thereof, as well as the great, and that even the lowest, when impassioned, raise their language; that the writing of prose is generally the plea and excuse of poverty of Genius." And some others being of the same opinion, I have now chang'd it all into metre.

> Fired is the Muse! and let the Muse be fired. Who's not in-
> flam'd, when what he speaks he feels? Young.

The introduction by the moderns of confidents, those friends in Tragedy, to whom the chief personages discover their secrets and situation, has been also objected to by critics. The discovery is indeed purposely made to the audience, and supplies the want of a chorus. But to speak in Monsieur Brumos's own stile: "If Homer, in his Epic poem, found a Patroclus necessary to his Achilles, and Virgil an Achates to Aeneas, such examples may well justify the Dramatic Poets in calling in the assistance of associates, who generally appear of more use than ornament to the piece." Besides, were it not for them, long and disgusting soliloquies must be innumerable, especially if there be any plot in the piece of either love, ambition, or conspiracy. In short, as he again says, "they are the mortar which forms the proper cement to fix the corner stones of the building."

But I declare, that the avoiding on the one hand, a style too high, as on the other, too mean and vulgar for the subject, or the persons concerned therein, has been a talk far more difficult to me than any of the best formed lines in either of my other Tragedies, so that I tremble at the thought of the reception this may meet with; and had it not been on account of the moral it inculcates, and the solicitation of some of my friends, I never should have published it.

PROLOGUE,

By Mr. R. Lewis,

Author of the Candid Philosopher, &c. &c.

The Muse prolific of a Vet'ran Bard Again brings forth;—but yet with labour hard. Nor is it strange, that such a Muse feels pain, When her child starts, like Pallas, from the brain, Arm'd at all points; when bold, she dares engage, With Truth's bright arms, the monsters of the age; When with just aim she points keen Satire's dart, And stabs the foul fiend GAMING to the heart. Yet has our Bard, to simple Nature true, Not brought up scenes of grandeur to your view; Not sought by magic arts to strike your eyes, Nor made the gods descend, or fiends arise: His plan is humble, and his fable plain, The town his scene, and artless is his strain: Yet in that strain some lambent sparks still glow Of that bright flame which shew'd Almeyda's woe, Which far-fam'd Tamor's Siege so well display'd, To fire each hero, and to charm each maid. Attend, ye Fair and Brave!—Our daring Bard Hopes in your smiles to meet his best reward. And you, ye Critics! if to censure bent, Think on this fact, and scorn the harsh intent; Our Bard would fain discordant things unite, As hard to reconcile as day and night: He strives within chaste Hymen's bands to draw The tuneful maids and sages of the law; Or, what's alike—nor think he means a joke— Melpomene to wed with old judge Coke. Yet still, if you'll not let his faults pass free, The Grecian rev'rence pay to sixty-three.

PERSONS OF THE DRAMA.

Men.

ANDREWS, merchant and banker. WILSON, GOODWIN, merchants, his neighbours. Lord BELMOUR, an English peer. Lord WESTON, nephew to lord BELMOUR. JEFFERSON, first clerk and cashier to Mr. ANDREWS. THOMAS, steward to Mr. ANDREWS.

Women.

Mrs. ANDREWS. Lady BELMOUR. CONSTANTIA, daughter to Mr. ANDREWS, by a former wife. LUCIA, her kinswoman. MARIA, waiting-woman to Mrs. ANDREWS, and wife to THOMAS.

Attendants and other servants, bailiffs, &c.

Scene, London.

THE FEMALE GAMSTER.

ACT I.

SCENE I. Mr. ANDREWS's house. Enter MARIA and THOMAS. MARIA. But why these moping, melancholy looks? Each eye observes and marks them now unseemly, Whilst every countenance but your's speaks joy, At the near wedding of our master's daughter. Sure none so well deserv'd this noble prize: And young lord Weston will be bless'd indeed. THOMAS. It has been countermanded. MARIA. What again? This is the second time. What can this mean? Then, his unusual absence, now a month, Nor any cause assign'd. THOMAS. Some accident. I know a truer flame was ne'er profess'd: A fondness which commenced in his apprenticeship, Here in this house, then but the late lord's nephew, Nor next in heirship to estate or title. MARIA. And sure all must approve his well-judg'd choice! In charms and virtues there are none surpass her. THOMAS. Heav'n grant my fears are groundless! but, Maria, To think on what of late I daily see, Afflicts my soul. MARIA. What is't your fears suggest? THOMAS. A wasted fortune and a sinking credit, With the near ruin of this worthy family; The thought materially concerns us both. MARIA. But, why again, should we distress ourselves For that we cannot help? THOMAS. Ungenerous thought! Duty and love and gratitude demand it. 'Twas here we met each other; here we wedded, And ever have receiv'd the kindest treatment. But what disturbs me most — I have been privy To matters which I should not have conceal'd From our good friend her father. MARIA. Think not of it. It is not possible to save them now. THOMAS. Would in his second marriage he had met With one more suited to his years and rank! MARIA. But are not all things for the better alter'd? Our house fill'd often with the best of company? THOMAS. The best saidst thou? O! no, the worst of all, A shameless crew of fashionable pillagers; So that this bank house, by their nightly riot, Might rather seem a rake-frequented tavern; And ruin is their sport. Is not each servant A worn-out victim to those midnight revels, Without a sabbath's rest? (For in these times, All sanctity is scoff'd at by the great, And heaven's just wrath defy'd.) An honest master, Scarcely a month beyond his fiftieth year, (Heart-rent with trouble at these sad proceedings,) Wears to the eye a visage of fourscore: Nor to be wondered at. MARIA. You dream too much. THOMAS. O! it is seen by all. Oft through his groves, With folded arms and downcast looks he saunters, Ev'n 'midst the dank inclemency of night. MARIA. You're too severe, too scrupulous; why, man, My mistress is a perfect saint, compar'd With some of those I formerly have serv'd. THOMAS. Her conduct has of late been foully censur'd. But I've disclos'd the whole to our kind neighbours Wilson and Goodwin, his most faithful friends— MARIA. For which ten thousand blisters scald your tongue! [Aside] THOMAS. Who are resolv'd (the task howe'er ungrateful) Quickly to lay his desp'rate state before him. MARIA. But pray, why should not we as well as others, Avail ourselves of something, whilst all's going? THOMAS. Think'st thou to tempt me by a thought so vile? No; I defy ev'n Envy's cankering tongue To brand me with the name of faithless steward Still steady to my trust, nor love, nor fear, Shall reason from my soul, its inbred honesty. What then would be the transport of the thought, That I, from wreck had sav'd this shatter'd bark, Though poverty and want were my reward! MARIA. I see you are as obstinate as usual, And still persist in your old-fashion'd ravings. Does not experience daily prove that wealth Alone gives honour; poverty disgrace? THOMAS. All this concerns this transient world alone; Nor is it worth a single moment's thought. A slender pittance, earn'd by honest industry, Surpasses mines of wealth acquir'd by fraud. MARIA. It cannot sure be wrong to make reprisals! Hath she not got in loan from us our earnings From time to time, nor heeds our pressing calls? THOMAS. Ay, as she wastes the honest tradesman's dues, Which from her husband she receives to pay. But would her crime be an excuse for ours? Were that the rule, 'twould be a desp'rate world. MARIA. 'Tis not a wonder he should be distress'd. Six months are scarcely past since one cashier, In whom you know he plac'd the highest confidence, Absconded with some thousands. THOMAS. So 'tis said, [Bell rings] But time will quickly shew the truth of all. MARIA. Heard you the bell? 'tis he, just come to town. THOMAS. And well he came so late, or he had met On their retreat, that group of restless rioters, Who day and night pursue this misled woman. [Bell rings again.] It is the bell again. I am resolv'd To speak my fears, receive them as he may. MARIA. Prithee, forbear till you revolve it further. [He, goes off] Doubtless she's daily plunging into ruin The poor infatuated man her husband, Whom fondness hath made blind to her misconduct. But I must hear what passes at this meeting; Wherefore, I'll to the closet next the chamber, Where usually they meet for private conference. [She goes off.]

SCENE II. Another room in Mr. ANDREWS's house. Mr. ANDREWS and THOMAS. ANDREWS. What strange disorder runs thro' all this house! It seems more like a place of midnight revelling, Than habitation of a sober family, And every servant in it looks a spectre. [A servant delivers Mr. ANDREWS a letter, which he reads; servant retires.] "This from your late unfortunate cashier, serves to inform you that he never wrong'd you; 'tis true, he was deficient much when he departed, yet, by that Power to whom all thoughts lie open! he knows not how it happened; but, if the present rumours are not false, your greatest foe is nearest to your heart." Such secret notices of late are frequent. When was this letter brought? THOMAS. 'Twas left last night. ANDREWS. Is my wife up? THOMAS. She's not long gone to rest. ANDREWS. Too much her practised course. Unthinking woman! Thus she precipitates our common ruin. [Aside.] Did not you tell me that my neighbour Wilson Had been enquiring for me here to-day? THOMAS. He was three times, and now I hear his voice. ANDREWS. 'Tis opportune; return when he departs. [THOMAS goes off] Enter WILSON. Welcome! thrice welcome! truest, best of friends. WILSON. I hope 'twill speedily be in my power, As 'tis my wish sincere, to give you joy On the most happy marriage of your daughter. Andrew. A thousand thanks! 'twas to have been to morrow, But is postponed a while. WILSON. There is no prize, Wealthy, or noble, which she doth not merit. ANDREWS. Again I thank my friend; but tell me wherefore, We meet not now as we were wont? time was When scarce a single day knew us asunder; Of late we're so for weeks. WILSON. Where lies the blame? You then were us'd to join your happy friends, In all their harmony and mirthful innocence; But you and yours have quite estrang'd yourselves, Scorning to mingle in our humble circles. ANDREWS. And is this mode of life to us peculiar? The tide of fashion, in these days of riot, Sweeps all before it that its torrent meets. WILSON. To our eternal shame! — All sense is fled, And ev'ry social pleasure with their virtues. Nor boast we more that wholesome plain economy Which made our ancestors so justly fam'd For honestly, and every gen'rous deed; But in its stead a splendid, wasteful vanity (Regardless of the toiler's hard-earn'd claims,) Pervades each rank, and all distinction levels: Too sure forerunners of the loss of freedom. ANDREWS. Your picture is as just as it is gloomy. But you can firmly stem th' infection's tide, And 'scape the censure we so justly merit. Yet you'd not blame your friend, if you knew all. [He walks to and fro.] WILSON. I cannot longer justify myself, To be a mute spectator of such ruin, As hourly threatens this respected family. [Aside.] To flatter, or conceal would ill become That friendship you have said you so esteem. My heart is open then, and can't acquit you. You've lost that fortitude you once possess'd. ANDREWS. O Wilson! I confess your charge is just. The truth is, I'm no longer master here, Nor of my family, nor of myself; And yet you may remember, no man liv'd More happily than I with my first wife. WILSON. She had all the virtues that adorn her sex. ANDREWS. And was withal of such a gentle nature, That I could ne'er conceive that ev'n in thought, She would impede or contradict my wish. WILSON. The loss was great. 'Tis now about ten years? ANDREWS.

Not more: you also know, that shortly after, (Full short indeed!) I wedded with the present. WILSON. Not with the approbation of your friends. Our women even then were greatly alter'd, Their manners as their education different. Their beauties too, are as their hearts deceitful, While art supplies the spoil of their excesses. I'm happy in the thoughts of being single. ANDREWS. Condemn not all for some; and prize their worth. By them we are refin'd; by them inspir'd; For them, we ev'ry toil and danger court, That lead to glory and make fame immortal. Trust me, my friend, there's no terrestrial blessing Equals the union of two souls in virtue. WILSON. Your wife was then but Young? ANDREWS. About sixteen, And I in years superiour to her father. Yet she appear'd of such congenial manners With my first wife, whose intimate she was, It led me to this early second marriage. And ev'n long after, such was her behaviour, That I insensibly forgot my loss; For tho' by birth and family allied, To several of the first in rank and fortune, Yet did not that the least affect her conduct, Which she still suited to our humbler station; A tender parent and a loving wife. WILSON. And such might have remain'd, had she not quit The innocent society of those, Who best were suited to her state in life. ANDREWS. O! 'tis most true; and I have often thought My happiness too great for long continuance. The toil, fatigue and numerous disappointments, (The sure attendants on a life of business) Were sooth'd and sweeten'd by the fond endearments, With which she met me in the hours of leisure. Oft hath she vow'd, that she despis'd the profit, How great soe'er, that sunder'd us at times. But all the halcyon days I once enjoy'd, Do but conspire to aggravate the misery, Which now quite weighs me down. WILSON. Nor is it strange. Your house is grown a nuisance to its neighbours, Where twice in every week, if not more frequent, A motley crowd at midnight hour assembles; Whose ruffian-like attendants in the street, Alarm the peaceful, and disturb their quiet. ANDREWS. I know, I feel it all. WILSON. Its inside too Is not less riotous; where this same medly Waste the whole night, destroying health and fortune, Of ev'ry social duty quite regardless. ANDREWS. They've been unseen by me. My health's weak state Will not admit my sleeping in the city; Whence also, I am often whole days absent; As my neglected finances disclose. Have you at any time beheld these scenes? WILSON. Once, on the invitation of your spouse. ANDREWS. Relate them, if not irksome. WILSON. At your instance. Then, the first object 'midst this wild assembly, (For such the night's proceedings fully prov'd it) That urg'd my wonder, was the heavy purses Which were display'd there, even by the women, Without remorse or shame. ANDREWS. Ay, there!—Proceed. WILSON. After the night had been near three part wasted, Full half the meeting more like spectres seem'd Than of this world. The clamour then grew great; Whilst ev'ry torturing passion of the foul Glar'd in the ghastly visages of several. Some grinn'd in rage, some tore their hair, whilst others, Upon their knees, with hands and eyes uplifted, In curses dar'd assail all-ruling Providence Under the varied names of Fate and Fortune. Nor is there one in the black list of crimes, Which these infernals seem'd not prompt to perpetrate, Whilst on a cast their trembling fortunes hung. ANDREWS. O Wilson! every passion, every power Of the great human soul are by this vice, This fatal vice of all, quite, quite absorb'd, Save those which its fell purposes excite! Oh! that most vile seducer lady Belmour! Wer't not for her, my wife had been a stranger To all those evils; I to all my misery. WILSON. But have our sex surrender'd their prerogative? Or have I liv'd to see the world revers'd? You are a man— ANDREWS. I know not what I am. Alas! my friend is stranger to these matters! When once a woman deviates from discretion, Setting her heart on every vain pursuit, No husband then rests master of his fate. Fond love no limit knows to its submission, Not more than beauty to its thirst for empire, Whose tears are not less pow'rful than its smiles. Nay, ev'n dislike, 'gainst reason, oft must yield, Whilst the mind's quiet is an object priz'd; So is the sex from its sweet purpose chang'd— WILSON. Your state then seems quite hopeless of relief? ANDREWS. O! could I wean her from this one sad vice! Wipe out this only speck in her rich volume! Then, all my woes should cease; then, would I write, In truth's fair characters, her matchless worth, Nor blush to boast the fondness of

my heart. WILSON. Your love admits some doubt. AN-
DREWS. My love of her!— — - WILSON. Ev'n so. Do you not
tamely see her, ev'ry day, Destroying wantonly her precious
health? But what is more — — —I shall proceed too far. AN-
DREWS. Go on, I am prepar'd. WILSON. Her reputation—
ANDREWS. Her reputation! WILSON. I have said it, AN-
DREWS. Heav'n! WILSON. It has not 'scap'd the busy tongue
of censure, Yet let appearances be what they may, I think
she's innocent. ANDREWS. What, innocent! Against appearances!—impossible. All sense disclaims the thought; these
neglected, Neglect of virtue is the sure attendant, And ev'n
the firmest may be then seduced;— 'Tis as the noon-day
plain.—Who? who's the villain? The murderer of my peace?
By heav'n! he dies. WILSON. Madness indeed! all may be
mere surmise; Wherefore, at present it will be most prudent,
To hush the sad ideas of suspicion. A little time must prove
its truth, or falsehood; Besides, the person charg'd is of high
rank. ANDREWS. O! there's no rank can sanctify such outrage. Lord Belmour! say— WILSON. Yes—he—or why that
name? ANDREWS. They nearly are a-kin—and yet of late
His visits have been rather more than usual. But have you
any proof for this your hint? WILSON. It is the current rumour of the neighbourhood, Else I should ne'er have dar'd to
wound your ear; But friendship urges the unpleasing task—
You tell me, you sleep mostly in the country? ANDREWS.
What then? he may, ev'n when I sleep in town, Pass nights
with her, and all unknown to me. WILSON. You puzzle me.
ANDREWS. 'Tis easily explain'd. For some time past we've
slept in separate chambers. For when she had exchang'd her
harmless life For the destructive course she now pursues,
Her hours became so late and so uncertain, My rest was quite
disturb'd. WILSON. Unhappy state! Have you discours'd her
calmly on these matters? Few of her sex possess superiour
talents. ANDREWS. Her temper is so chang'd, so sour'd of
late, Which with her sad misconduct still increases; And she
so prides herself on her alliances, And the caresses of her
vain associates, That neither I, nor her neglected children,
Dare ev'n attempt the least discourse with her. Did you know
all, 'twould rend your tender heart. [He pauses a while, then

walks about much disturbed.] WILSON. He has abundance more to hear of yet; Two bills this very day, went off unpaid, A stroke too fatal, e'er to be recover'd. [Aside.] Affliction is heav'n's trial of our patience, As of its love sure proof; and oft' our benefit. ANDREWS. Can you continue friend to such lost fortune? WILSON. How it would grieve me could you even doubt it! The surest test of friendship is affliction. 'Tis then, the faithful heart displays itself, Whilst vain professors vanish in the gloom. ANDREWS. Tell me—Oh tell me! what would you advise? WILSON. Against we meet on the Exchange to-day, I will revolve it well. ANDREWS. Reward your goodness heav'n! [WILSON goes off.] Re-enter THOMAS. Oh what a fatal change in my affairs! Have you observ'd it, Thomas, yet been silent? THOMAS. I almost wish I knew not how to answer: But since it is his will I must obey. [Aside.] Dare then your faithful servant speak some truths, With which his heart is full? ANDREWS. What prevents you? THOMAS. I dare not—yet—[aside] suppose 'twere of a wife, So lov'd, so doted on?— ANDREWS. Prithee, proceed. THOMAS. Then know, last night, that as I lay awake, And hearing near the compting-house a noise, I rose, and in the dark mov'd softly towards it; When I (unseen by her) beheld her passing Quickly from thence, and in her hands a light, And key, with which she op'd the iron chest. ANDREWS. [After some pause] Good heav'n! that she could injure me so deeply — — — My credit— — —but I cannot bear to expose her! Means have been us'd to stop all further mischief, On some suspicions of mine own before. So for the present, must appear to doubt it. [Aside.] [To THOMAS] For this, I owe you my most grateful thanks. I've ever found you faithful to my interest; Yet, as your zeal may have alarm'd your fears, Speak not of this, until I weigh it further, Not even to your wife. THOMAS. I shall obey. [THOMAS goes off] ANDREWS. What an unhappy man!—It is impossible— I ne'er knew one in ev'ry thought more pure Than she was once— and now to be so chang'd— I will not see her more—and yet—O heav'n!— 'Tis demonstration only can convince me. Ah! lovely woman, didst thou ne'er design But in thy proper sphere alone to shine, Using with modesty each winning art,

To fix, as well as captivate the heart, Love's purest flame might gild the nuptial days, And Hymen's altars then for ever blaze.

ACT II.

SCENE I. An apartment in Mr. ANDREWS's house. Mrs. ANDREWS and MARIA. Mrs. ANDREWS. I'm quite amaz'd at what you have related. [She walks to and fro much agitated.] MARIA. I must not now discover, how her husband Receiv'd the tidings of a secret key: She would not rest, until reveng'd of mine. [Aside.] Mrs. ANDREWS. Can you now help me? I am much distress'd. MARIA. You know I am devoted to your service. Mrs. ANDREWS. So I have ever thought. — Heav'n! what a state! Compell'd to sooth ev'n those my soul abhors. [Aside.] MARIA. Madam, I'm griev'd to see your spirits sinking. But hear me, and I think I can propose A scheme by which it may be so contriv'd, As to retort this charge on your fair character, Cruel as false, respecting the lord Belmour, On your base neighbour Wilson, the inventer, With honour to yourself. Mrs. ANDREWS. What, and he innocent? MARIA. Hath he not wrong'd you? — — — beyond all redress? Labour'd to blast your spotless fame for ever, Whilst you are innocent? Mrs. ANDREWS. Yet much to blame. [Aside.] MARIA. Wherefore, your honour calls aloud for vengeance. Mrs. ANDREWS. True; his harsh, cruel, groundless, information Hath to my poor mind's peace been most injurious. MARIA. It is the only means I can devise, At once to wipe away this foul aspersion, And all the other mischiefs that may follow. Mrs. ANDREWS. But how, I pray? none bear more fair repute. MARIA. Yet vers'd in gallantry. Mrs. ANDREWS. So I have heard. MARIA. That answers well; suppose then, in a letter, You mention earnestly, his having made Some overtures injurious to your honour, And should he persevere, that you'll disclose This breach of truth and friendship to your husband? Then, let this letter, as it were by chance, Fall in my master's way. — Consider this. Mrs. ANDREWS. [Pauses] A most ingenious thought! — but to pursue it — [Pauses again.] Shall I at such dark villainy connive! — Are there no means to 'scape the tongue of calumny, But by imbibing her infectious breath, And blasting innocence with sland'rous falsehood? Chang'd howsoe'er I be, yet my soul

shudders Ev'n at the thought of an unjust revenge— I ne'er
could reconcile it to myself. MARIA. Again I say, your own
defence demands it. It is the sole resource you have to save
you. Mrs. ANDREWS. I am myself the cause of all these miseries. [Aside.] I see great difficulties in this matter. MARIA. I,
not any—do you but write this letter; The rest be mine—but
soft!—my master's voice— Mrs. ANDREWS. What shall I do?
I would not meet him now. MARIA. You must not, till our
purpose is effected. Be not distress'd—I'll urge a fit excuse.
So, to your chamber, and prepare the letter, No patience can
submit to such indignities. [Goes off.] Mrs. ANDREWS. I
dread the very thoughts of this—and yet— To rest beneath so
vile an accusation— It cannot—must not be—I should be
false, And to myself unjust—and then, revenge Upon this
slanderer—I'm much perplex'd. [Goes off.]

SCENE II. Changes to another room in Mr. ANDREWS's
house. Enter Mr. ANDREWS, leaning on THOMAS and another person; CONSTANTIA attending him. THOMAS. This
outward room is large, the air more free. ANDREWS.
Faint!—very faint!—support me to yon couch. [They seat him
on a couch.] I hop'd at length heav'n's goodness had deter-
min'd To give my soul its so long wish'd-for peace. CON-
STANTIA. Of late, these fierce attacks give fresh alarm. Pre-
serve him, heav'n,—O sir! behold your daughter.— AN-
DREWS. Tir'd nature hath got respite for a while, Yet weak-
en'd much—my final rest is near. [To the servants.] Withdraw awhile; but wait within a call. Constantia! stay; come
nearer to your father. Give me your hand, I wish a private
conference On somewhat of much moment ere we part.
CONSTANTIA. You make your daughter happy; for of late,
I've thought, you did not see me with that pleasure To which
I had been us'd; I, therefore fear'd, You some distress had
met, or that Constantia, Had witlessly, (when some ill fate
presided,) The best of parents and of friends offended. AN-
DREWS. You never did; it is against your nature. You've ever
been affectionate as dutiful; But the postponing thus a second
time (And on lord Weston's side) the purpos'd wedding,
Which all must say, our station weigh'd with his, Besides his

princely qualities of mind, Would highly honour us, disturbs me much: Yet, wou'd I hope, th' affections of your heart Are not so fix'd upon this noble youth, you cou'd not wean them thence, shou'd it be fit. CONSTANTIA. What is't I hear! undone! be still, my heart! [Aside.] Hath not a letter, sir, disclos'd the cause? ANDREWS. Such letter I receiv'd, yet it is said, His uncle, the lord Belmour, hath of late, Spoken of this, to which he once consented, In terms of discontent; which, if as told, I would to the alliance of an emperour, Prefer the badge of want. CONSTANTIA. [She kneels] O most indulgent! Ever-honour'd sir! let not a thought for me Distress your tenderness. Heav'n be my judge! That did my faithful heart approve him more (If possible) than I have truly told you, And that its choice was not with your assent, My task should be, to tear it thence for ever. And, but I know lord Weston has a soul, Possess'd of every virtue heav'n bestows, I wou'd far rather wed in mine own rank, Where truth and happiness are oft'ner found, Than midst the glaring grandeur of the great. ANDREWS. Come to thy father's arms, thou sweet resemblance Of the perfections of your much-lov'd mother; A loss each day felt more — yet, my Constantia, What tho' your charms and virtue shou'd surpass All that e'er center'd in a virgin frame, To be the choice of this exalted youth Causes a thousand fears in my fond heart. CONSTANTIA. O sir! how you alarm me! heav'n! what fears? ANDREWS. Constantia singled out, preferr'd to numbers Of the first rank, who would exult to win him, Will rouse up ev'ry baneful blast of envy, Perfections such as thine ne'er 'scape malignity. CONSTANTIA. The example of that honour to her sex, My dear lost mother, with the wholesome lessons Instill'd by you, will so direct my steps, I may those blasts escape your fondness fears. ANDREWS. Yet, should this change in your condition happen, This also treasure in your mind; that man, As in his frame, so is his spirit rough; Whilst your more tender sex was form'd by heav'n, To sooth those cares, which from his state still flow, With winning grace, and smooth life's rugged paths. That she who best submits will surest reign; In youth be idolized, in age revered. But when perverse contention marks her conduct, And passion's transitory joys are pall'd, The past offence will to the mind recur, And all that once had charm'd be quite forgot. CONSTANTIA. Good heav'n! of two such parents make me worthy. Enter MARIA. ANDREWS. Some message from my wife — withdraw awhile. CONSTANTIA. [As she goes off] Alas! I fear some deep distress affects him. ANDREWS. Where is your mistress? MARIA. In her chamber, sir. ANDREWS. Go tell her I am here, and wish to see her. MARIA. Good sir! she has been greatly indispos'd: But somewhat eas'd, was in a friendly slumber, Till rous'd at hearing that some sudden ailment Had just now seiz'd you, she dispatch'd me hither, And most impatient waits for my return With tidings of your health, to her so precious. ANDREWS. This woman is so hackney'd in all baseness, That even truth from her would be disgrac'd. [Aside.] Had her condition far exceeded all Your seeming tender fears; or did I hear The peal of her death bell, I shou'd not wonder. Was she not up all night? Was ever seen Such rapid havock as this life of riot Spreads o'er her bloom, which ev'ry art abash'd, Now vainly practis'd to repair its ruin! Sad victim to the world's most baleful fashions! MARIA. Some friends staid later here last night than usual. But if you knew how much she's indispos'd, I'm sure 'twould pierce your heart; as I well know, You love her tenderly, as she does you. ANDREWS. Wou'd I had lov'd her less, or ne'er had seen her! Retire awhile, I pray — I wou'd be private. MARIA. [As she goes off] We now shall execute the scheme I plann'd. ANDREWS. I am the veriest wretch that breathes the air, And nought but desperation is before me.

[A Servant BOY enters hastily at a different door, as if passing to another room, with a letter in his hand, starts, (as if at seeing his master) and affects to conceal the letter.] ANDREWS. You seem confus'd — What paper's that? BOY. 'Tis, sir — 'tis a letter — ANDREWS. From whom? and to whom? BOY. From, sir, — Why, 'tis — [He seizes the boy's hand, who drops the letter, and whilst his master is taking it up, runs off.] ANDREWS. Ha! what, gone off! how guilt betrays itself! Here is some secret scheme — 'tis in my wife's hand. The superscription to my old friend Wilson — I never yet approv'd of opening letters By any, save by those to whom address'd; But to detect deceit, such means are just; And here it seems, as matters were on foot, With which, 'tis meant I should not be acquainted. Besides, of late, I have at times surpriz'd them in close and intimate discourse together; When, it now strikes me, they seem'd much confounded. Upon the whole, I think I ought to read it: Necessity demands the doubtful deed. [He opens and reads the letter.] "Sir, I might have thought the repulse you so lately receiv'd, with the declaration I then made of acquainting my husband with your conduct, would have deterred you from ever making any further attempt. — How fatal might the consequences prove should I discover your behaviour to him? Is this your friendship? Know, base man! that whatever my follies and indiscretions may be in other respects, there is not any distress shall lead me to an act against the honour of Elizabeth Andrews." Am I awake! or is this all a dream? My friend — seduce my wife? it cannot be! [Looks again on the letter.] It surely is her hand — it must be so. She's now but in her prime, and few so beautiful — Then his strict charge this morning, not to mention What he himself had told me was reported Of her and the lord Belmour, with this letter, Are proofs which make this matter nearly certain. What ruin is at hand! — — — [He pauses.] Enter MA-RIA hastily. Woman, your business? MARIA. My lady, sir, is up, and begs to see you; Or she will wait on you. ANDREWS. I choose the latter. [She goes off.] How wond'rous condescending of a sudden! Shou'd this be a true charge in this dread letter, All he has mentioned of her and lord Belmour, May be a base invention for his purpose — Yet, may not both be true? — distracting state! Enter Mrs. ANDREWS. [He in profound thought, and not observing her.] Mrs. ANDREWS. He heeds me not. The letter strongly works. [Aside.] I've been inform'd, sir, that you wish'd to see me. You seem disturb'd; acquaint me with the cause. ANDREWS. Forbear to question me. I am not well. Mrs. ANDREWS. You yield too much to melancholy thoughts. ANDREWS. True — Melancholy hath been long my portion; As I've too long the fatal cause conceal'd: But ev'ry duty now, to heaven, to you, To my poor children, to myself, all, all Demand it from the husband and the father, That you, oh! you, are the sole, fatal cause. [She offers to withdraw, he shuts the door.] Mrs. ANDREWS. How your looks scare me! what have I committed? ANDREWS. O! many things you should not have committed. To number all the mischiefs which your conduct, Your most misguided conduct hath induc'd On those, to whom, each law divine and human Had bound you in affection's strongest ties, Were but a needless waste of time and speech. [Aside] Heav'n! what contempt and scorn her looks betray! O Gaming! cursed vice! parent of all! How callous grow the hearts of all thy votaries! And how hast thou this once soft bosom chang'd! Nor is her form less alter'd than her mind. [Turning to her] Perverse and obstinate! as adders deaf! Mrs. ANDREWS. Your words are not unheard. ANDREWS. It matters not; Without due heed, 'twere speaking to the winds. Have you yet thought, how you could bear the change, The bitter change from affluence to poverty, Which ev'ry want will bring to your remembrance? We both must in one ruin be involv'd. Mrs. ANDREWS. I know no life I lead that is not suited To what I am entitled by my birth: An honour, sir, of which you seem insensible. ANDREWS. True honour only lies in virtuous deeds. But had you been the daughter of a prince, 'Twere fit you suitably demean'd yourself, To that condition you had freely chosen. Mrs. ANDREWS. By gloomy minds, and years by ailments sour'd, Remembring not past seasons in themselves, Ev'n pleasures innocent are deem'd offence. ANDREWS. No — no; it lies not in their decent use; 'Tis the extreme that constitutes the fault, By which, ev'n Virtue's sacred self might err; But they who break a single law, would others, If lured alike; so violate the whole. Mrs. ANDREWS. Ha! is it come to this? arraign my virtue? ANDREWS. This quick impatience is self-accusation. I have not even hinted at it yet. Mrs. ANDREWS. Whilst I am conscious of my own heart's innocence, I scorn the censure of a slanderous world; It cannot injure me. ANDREWS. Soft! have a care. No virtue with that thought is safe a moment. O! 'tis a jewel of such brilliant lustre, And so resistless wins the admiration, That even vice, in its appearance mansk'd, Pays homage at its shrine. Mrs. ANDREWS. What is't I hear? I see th' ill-natur'd purpose of your summons. But who are they, sir, who have dar'd traduce me? Some, it is like, of your low-rank'd associates? ANDREWS. This war of words is wandering from the purpose. Now, mark me well—the man who dares insult A woman's modesty, must have descry'd Somewhat in her behaviour that would warrant Such outrage of abuse.—Is this your hand? [Shewing her the letter.] Mrs. ANDREWS. Let me see it. [He gives her the letter, which she reads hastily, then tears it to pieces.] Now, let me tell you, sir, 'Twas a base action to unclose this letter, Or any other not to you address'd. What a curs'd hellish plot hath here been schem'd Against my peace! oh! oh! Maria—oh! [She faints upon the sofa.] Enter MARIA. MARIA. Alas! alas! my poor lady! good sir! What hath she done to merit this unkindness? You've always been the tenderest of husbands. ANDREWS. Forbear this idle talk; attend your mistress. [Aside] What fool was I to trust her with this letter! Yet, why was she so hasty to destroy it? Heav'n! in what deep perplexities I'm plung'd! [He goes off.] Mrs. ANDREWS. What! gone! Leave me in the sad seeming state In which I call myself!—and unconcern'd! Would I had died before I wrote that letter! Desperate act! I knew not what I did. MARIA. Madam, despair not; this will soon blow over, You're young and beauteous; he, in his decline. You can command him, as best suits your pleasure; But let not scruples rule you at this crisis: In my poor judgment, 'twould undo us all. Consult your friend, the faithful lady Belmour; None can advise you better on this subject. Mrs. ANDREWS. O! but Maria, this is not the whole. My ill success at play for some time past, Hath far exceeded all hath yet befall'n me: This hurried me to borrow of lord Belmour A thousand pieces, which, with the several sums I've lost to him (not small), must now be paid; But above all,—ill fate! is the discovery Of the false key to my wrong'd husband's chest: Which must be so; as other locks are fix'd On it, and every door that leads thereto. MARIA. The work this, of my old officious husband. [Walks apart and pauses.] Now for due vengeance for the killing flights, That youth, the scornful Jefferson, hath cast On me, and my ill-fated fondness for him. [Returning.] What think you of a further application To the cashier; your worthy friend young Jefferson? Mrs. ANDREWS. I cannot: he already hath assur'd me, He dares not venture to supply me further. MARIA. I doubt not but he told you so; and yet, My hopes are surety still for his compliance. There is no danger he'd not risk to serve you. Mrs. ANDREWS. Whence comes this zeal? MARIA. From a passion for you, As violent perhaps, as e'er possess'd The heart of man, and which he cannot hide. You surely must have seen it? It destroys him. Mrs. ANDREWS. I have, 'tis true, observ'd him much confus'd At times I spoke to him; but this, I thought, Might have proceeded from a bashful modesty, As I conceive his readiness to serve me, Did from a generous spirit to oblige. MARIA. I tell you, madam, 'tis the height of fondness. A fever, that he lately had, in which His ceaseless ravings were of you, confirm'd 'it. He shuns all company, neglects his food, And wanders often, as would one insane. Mrs. ANDREWS. Astonishment! MARIA. He cannot quit the house His 'prenticeship has full two years expir'd, And twice he hath prepar'd him for the Indies. I know the inmost secrets of his soul: Besides, of late, he's often much intoxicated, Who was before the paragon of temperance. Do but consent to let me call him hither; One look from you will banish every fear, Unlock each chest, and lay its stores before you. Mrs. ANDREWS. Stop! at your peril stop! the very thought Chills my whole blood—I'd perish first in want. MARIA. Then you must quit your honourable friends, And live for ever in forlorn obscurity. But pardon me, if I've been too officious. Mrs. ANDREWS. My present calls require at least a thousand: For though my fund be not quite exhausted, Fortune hath made me bankrupt yet to numbers. 'Tis true, that many are far more my debtors, Yet are not all like me in payment punctual. But I will instant haste to lady Belmour, My faithful counsel in the time of trouble. MARIA. As I could wish. Mrs. ANDREWS. Then for awhile withdraw. [MARIA goes off.] How dreadful now, is ev'n a moment's privacy! How different from those happy hours of innocence, When my sweet little ones were prattling round me, With a fond husband and a tender father, Pouring his blessings upon them and me! But now I can no more endure to see them, Than I can bear to

look into myself. How often hath he said, "One hour's remorse Outweighs whole years of transitory joys!" How true
he spoke! but wherefore these reflections? When every mischief hath been done already, And cannot be recall'd! Re-
enter MARIA. MARIA. Madam, the coach. Mrs. ANDREWS.
Be not you absent; I shall soon return, And may have business of some moment with you. MARIA. I fear we have too
much on hand already. [Aside.] [They go off.]

SCENE III. Another room in Mr. ANDREWS's house. JEF-
FERSON alone. JEFFERSON. My actions must at length fall
heavy on me, And crush me at a blow: but oh! this passion,
This fruitless passion, I've so long indulg'd For this enchanting woman, drives me on, Alas! from one transgression to
another, And I deceive myself. — Ha! here's Maria. Wou'd I
cou'd shun her! as of late her visits Have been more frequent
than occasions warrant. Yet much she hath profess'd herself
my friend, And my heart's secret won. Enter MARIA. MA-
RIA. I disturb you. JEFFERSON. Why to speak truly, I had
just now sought Some private intercourse with mine own
heart. MARIA. Of late, I think you use too much of that. But
if you knew from whom I am a messenger, I also think, I
should not be unwelcome. But I'll withdraw. JEFFERSON.
No, speak your business quickly. MARIA. Alas! my poor
mistress! JEFFERSON. What of her? speak — — — MARIA.
Fortune has been of late to adverse to her, And she's become
indebted to such numbers, I fear she can no more appear in
publick, But must retire, unless your goodness serves her.
She often speaks with gratitude of Jefferson: Did you but see
in what distress she languishes, You'd hazard worlds to minister relief. JEFFERSON. Full well you know, how I'm inclin'd
to serve her; But her demands encrease with my compliance,
And I have injur'd much the best of masters. I know no other
banker cou'd support it. MARIA. Most happy youth! there
does not live another, Of whom my mistress would have
sought these favours. O! cou'd I venture, I could say much
more. — Thus far however, I'll be bold to utter; That were our
worthy master gone to rest, (And all observe he's every day
declining) You are the only man her heart would choose. —

But I have gone too far. JEFFERSON. Transporting sounds!
My soul is all attention!—Pray proceed. MARIA. I cannot—
O! I must not. JEFFERSON. Why? MARIA. Her honour. JEF-
FERSON. Say, are you truly serious in this matter? Or, but
amusing me with idle hopes? MARIA. Pray have you ever
found me such a trifler? JEFFERSON. I cannot say I have, and
yet— — MARIA. Yet, what? JEFFERSON. Her virtue! MA-
RIA. Why you are virtuous, yet cannot avoid This passion for
the loveliest of women: Nor may she be insensible to you. No
youth more wins our sex's admiration. Among the rest, the
beauteous, gentle Lucia, In secret languishes: it is too plain:
Though ev'ry art be practis'd to conceal it. JEFFERSON. Forbear this now. None prize her virtues more: Nor am I to her
outward charms insensible. But when the heart is to one object wedded, No lure can win it thence.— — —You flatter me?
MARIA. I don't.—You under-prize yourself.—View this.—
JEFFERSON. View what? [Eagerly] MARIA. It is a locket
with her precious hair, Which she has sent by me. Refuse it
not. JEFFERSON. Refuse it!—O! whilst life exists I'll wear it,
Close to that heart which is for ever hers. I am all ecstacy, de-
licious woman! [He kisses it.] MARIA. [Aside.] A lucky hit,
and works as I could wish. JEFFERSON. Gratefully thank her
for the precious token. MARIA. And now as to her present
exigencies? JEFFERSON. To what may they amount? MA-
RIA. About a thousand. JEFFERSON. 'Tis quite impossible.
MARIA. Less will not do. JEFFERSON. Besides the mischief I
have done my master, I stand myself upon the verge of ruin.
MARIA. Were you to see her, you'd not lose a moment In this
last act, so be yourself the messenger. JEFFERSON. First, tell
her then, that she shall be supply'd, Let the event be fatal as it
may. MARIA. Most gen'rous youth! she shall know all your
goodness. [She goes off.] JEFFERSON. How quickly every
resolution vanishes! And how am I now chang'd from what I
was! Like some weak skiff, that for a while had stood Safe on
the tranquil bosom of the flood; Until at length, the mountain
torrents sweep Its faint resistance headlong to the deep,
Where in large gulps the foamy brine it drinks, And in the
dread abyss for ever sinks. [Exit.]

ACT III.

SCENE I. A chamber in lord BELMOUR's house. Lady BEL-MOUR at her toilet, her Waiting-woman attending. Lady BELMOUR. How pale I look! ATTENDANT. My lady rose too early. Lady BELMOUR. Why, what's the time? AT-TENDANT. 'Tis past the noon, but it is scarce four hours Since you lay down to rest. [A tap at the door] Lady BEL-MOUR. Who can this be? [The ATTENDANT goes to the door and returns.] ATTENDANT. 'Tis Mrs. Andrews, mad-am, in her chariot. Lady BELMOUR. What, at this hour?— and yet in truth no wonder, That thus her rest's disturb'd. It would require The wealth of India to support her losses. And were she now possess'd of all its stores, I and my friends cou'd rid her of the burthen. Perhaps, she comes to pay me the five hundred I won of her, when last we play'd together? Or with the flattering hopes to make reprisals? So I may dou-ble it before we part: For she's unskill'd enough to lose a mil-lion. Away!—I'll wait her in the damask chamber. [They go off different ways.]

SCENE II. Changes to another apartment. Lady BELMOUR alone. Enter Mrs. ANDREWS. Lady BELMOUR. My dearest Andrews! I rejoice to see you. Mrs. ANDREWS. I always found you friendly and obliging. Lady BELMOUR. But why this gloom on that angelic face? Why not as sprightly as you us'd to be? Surely you'll not conceal the cause from me, Whose wishes for you are sincere as earnest! Mrs. AN-DREWS. How happy am I in this honour'd favour! You know my loss at play for some time past Hath been prodigious; it hath reach'd my husband. Lady BELMOUR. Were I in your case, that should not disturb me. Is not the jealous dotard twice your age? Such incidents shou'd more confirm my em-pire. Nay, my offence shou'd be his accusation, Nor wou'd I rest until he shou'd acknowledge The fault was his, not mine; so, rouse your spirits. Mrs. ANDREWS. Impossible, I've in-jur'd him too deeply; Have lost with his esteem, his love for ever. Lady BELMOUR. Then farewel further intercourse between us. [Aside] Despond not thus, all will be well again. I think you owe me just five hundred pieces? Yet let not that disturb you in the least: It may be in your power to pay me soon. Mrs. ANDREWS. I would not forfeit your regard and friendship, For fifty times the sum. Lady BELMOUR. Imagine not, That I cou'd doubt your honour, were it thousands. Your strict and constant perseverance in it, Has won you the esteem and love of all; And to convince you of my high opinion, I'll hazard this five hundred with you now. The day is early yet. Mrs. ANDREWS. O press me not; My mind's too-much distress'd with what has happen'd; But I have brought the honourable debt. [She takes out several notes from a pocket-book.] These make the whole, I think. Lady BELMOUR. Most honour'd friend! But may I trespass on your gen'rous spirit? Your stock I see, is not a little weighty. Cou'd you supply me with five hundred more For a few hours? I have no doubt to treble them, At a small party, I expect this instant: And I'll repay them gratefully this evening At lady Meldmay's, where we are to meet. I, and three more this morning hold a bank; In which, if you wou'd choose to share a chance, Fortune perhaps might favour you this way. Mrs. ANDREWS. Not now; but here's the further sum you wish for; And fail not to repay it as you promise. 'Tis but a part of what I owe to others. Lady BELMOUR. I wou'd not disappoint you for the world. My obligations are beyond expression. Grant heav'n, your present troubles quickly vanish. Mrs. ANDREWS. And may you meet the fortune which you hope for! [She goes off.] Lady BELMOUR. 'Tis wonderful, how she acquires all this. Her husband's ruin'd, my dissipated lord, Most lavishly, I hear, supplies her wants; Whilst even for domestic calls his purse Is niggardly unclos'd; and what he spares, Must be in strictest mode accounted for: Nor does he know a pleasure, absent from her. To keep this sum then, were but fair reprisals. [Exit.]

SCENE III. Mr. ANDREWS's house. Mr. ANDREWS and THOMAS. ANDREWS. What monsters trust will make us when we yield Our reason to its rage, and let it rule! My neighbour! my companion! Oh! the man, Whom I to serve, would have risk'd every blessing To seek to wound me in the tenderest point! Then, under friendship's show masking his treachery, Endeavour falsely to accuse another— Most infernal villain! THOMAS. 'Tis impossible. Say, is there one of more exalted virtues? Or one who so esteems and honours you? ANDREWS. Oh! my wife's letter proves beyond all question, This breach of friendship, gratitude and honour. THOMAS. All forgery. ANDREWS. She did not deny it. THOMAS. Where is it? ANDREWS. I have it not, she tore it. THOMAS. Tore it! how got she it? ANDREWS. It matters not. THOMAS. There's something more in this, than yet you know of. ANDREWS. If any thing by chance hath reach'd your ear, Against the safety ev'n of an enemy, Stain not your fair repute with the foul secret. The faithful tongue will utter what the heart In justice prompts, though death were the event. THOMAS. Then, sir, the letter is a black contrivance. And would you now forgive this tell-tale honesty, I shou'd not hesitate to name the forger. ANDREWS. These intermissions aggravate the misery. THOMAS. Prepare then for the shock. It was your wife. Boldly I speak the truth; for much she's wrong'd, If since she has been link'd with those high miscreants, Who, whilst they plunder, hold her in derision, Her foul's not ripe for ev'ry desp'rate project. [ANDREWS walks about much disturb'd.] Patience, good sir! I rest not on suspicion. ANDREWS. Audacious wretch, away!—quick, shun my rage! THOMAS. I meant you well. [Aside as he goes off.] How piteous is his case! [Exit.] ANDREWS. How can I meet him, and we both survive it! Dread interval! would I had ne'er been born. [Goes off.]

SCENE IV. Mr. ANDREWS's house. Mrs. ANDREWS and MARIA. Mrs. ANDREWS. Well, I believe if all my debts were paid, I ne'er should hazard more. MARIA. And so return To the dull, lonely life you once pursued? Forbid it your good angel! 'twould destroy you. Mrs. ANDREWS. O! but that life, Maria, was estrang'd To those anxieties which haunt me now. I cannot bear to be alone a moment. MARIA. For that good reason, act like lady Belmour; Like her be resolute, and scorn despair. Enter a SERVANT. SERVANT. Lord Belmour, madam, tenders his respects. Mrs. ANDREWS. [Aside.] How I dread these visits! Besides, of late, He hath been more particular than usual; So that it hath become the general notice. [To the Servant.] Withdraw awhile. [To MARIA.] I will not be at home. MARIA. What, not to him? That gallant, gen'rous nobleman! your friend! Mrs. ANDREWS. A creditor for more than I can pay. MARIA. Bless us! where are your boasted gains of late, And where the sum you just receiv'd from Jefferson? Mrs. ANDREWS. Of late, I have miss'd notes for several sums. Mar. I doubt she suspects me. [Aside.] Madam, 'tis like, You've lent them to some friends? Mrs. ANDREWS. Of this again. Have you yet rais'd the money on my jewels? MARIA. The broker thinks the pledge is not sufficient. Mrs. ANDREWS. For three thousand! they cost that sum twice told. MARIA. He'll not lend more than two. Mrs. ANDREWS. I must submit. [Aside.] Shameful return this to the gen'rous donor! Part was his present on our bridal day, And part the day, he bore the city's honours. He thought he never could enough adorn me. MARIA. But we forget — his lordship waits admission. Mrs. ANDREWS. I cannot see him, — yet, shou'd I refuse it, As my curs'd stars have destin'd me his debtor, He may, perhaps, conceive, it want of honour. MARIA. He scorns such thoughts; ev'n in his younger days, as in his mien, so in all noble deeds, Fair rumour tells, he was surpass'd by none. Mrs. ANDREWS. Say, is your master in the house? MARIA. No, madam. Mrs. ANDREWS. Well then, this once. — How I abhor myself! [MARIA goes off.] Enter Lord BELMOUR. Lord BELMOUR. How does my charming creditor this morning? Mrs. ANDREWS. Your debtor, I suppose you mean, my lord? Lord BELMOUR. Thou never was't my debtor. I'm thy slave; And in the pleasing chains would live for ever. To view that lovely form! those radiant eyes, And listen to the language of those lips! What sum can be a recompense for these O! that such matchless, such resistless beauty, Shou'd be condemn'd to the cold arms of age Or one of vulgar breed! — 'tis — Oh! it is — Mrs. ANDREWS. I know not what you mean. You talk in mystery. [He attempts to take her hand, at which she seems very uneasy, withdrawing it.] My lord, I must beseech you to desist, Or I must hence retire. Lord BELMOUR. But hear me first. This is a free discharge of all demands. [Produces a paper] This other writing binds me, as your debtor, In two thousand. [Produces another paper] Mrs. ANDREWS. I see his base designs. He seeks to take advantage of my wants. [Aside] I need no further proofs of your intentions. I have already heard too much. [She walks to and fro much disorder'd.] Lord BELMOUR. Too much! 'Tis strange! what have you heard? that I do love, Admire, adore you, O! beyond all utterance; But why conceive, that I intend you injury? Were my possessions as the globe extensive, You might command the whole, as you may him, Who lives, or dies, as you shall smile, or frown. Mrs. ANDREWS. Into what mischiefs do you mean to plunge me? Or wherefore do you dare insult me thus? Is it because I'm wedded to a citizen, (Forgetting that I am of your own kindred) That you these liberties presume? Know, sir, That through the world, an honest British trader Esteem and honour meets. But, were I lower Than vanity directs you to conceive me, And you of the first rank; where freedom reigns, You have no right to offer me such insult. Lord BELMOUR. Talk not of rank to one who loves as I do; The pride of kings beneath those eyes might languish, And prostrate thus, and trembling wait their sentence. [He falls on his knees, seizes her hand, which she forces from him.] Mrs. ANDREWS. What have you seen in my deportment, sir, To warrant this intrusion? 'tis unworthy. Lord BELMOUR. Will you not then vouchsafe one glance of pity? Is there no ray of hope; no room for pardon? O, inexorable! Mrs. ANDREWS. Protect me, heav'n! [Aside] Sir, at your peril, speak to me again. Lord BELMOUR. Teach, teach me first, how this devoted heart, Shall gain its freedom, or forget its fondness. That voice conveys such rapture to my soul, That I would hear it, though 'twere sure perdition. Mrs. ANDREWS. These hackney'd phrases, use to those they suit To me, they are accumulated insults. [He rises.] Lord BELMOUR. Forego such thoughts; I, nothing meant but honour. My wife and I, having resolv'd to sunder, (For without love we met, and so have liv'd,) Hope ev'ry moment our divorce for ever; When both may wed again, as each best likes; A practice now full easily accomplish'd. Then, that your husband's fate is near its period, 'Tis said, some recent symptoms have pronounc'd Wherefore, it soon may be my happy lot, To make thee partner of my rank and fortune, As thou'rt already empress of my heart. —Accept then, I beseech thee, these small tokens. [He gives her the papers, which she, in great confusion, insensibly takes.] And now with that sweet breath, surpassing far The spicy perfume of the budding rose, Pronounce the sentence of my life, or death. Mrs. AN-DREWS. To what an abject state am I reduc'd! The time has been, I'd not have heard a king Discourse me thus. [Aside.]—I charge you, sir, desist. Lord BELMOUR. I find 'tis vain to press my suit at present, An humour this, to which 'twere better yield. Best flatter it. [Aside.]—O! I am quite abash'd. Your merited rebukes so awe my soul, That I shall live from this day forth in penitence, And adoration of your heav'nly virtues: Let me then read in thy relenting eye My peace restor'd, or seal my final doom! Mrs. ANDREWS. Your future conduct must determine it. Lord BELMOUR. Permit me then, I pray— [He seizes her hand, and kisses it.] We are to meet At lady Meldmay's drawing-room to-night; Till then—[Aside as he goes off.]—The prize is mine. She now must yield. Mrs. ANDREWS. Are these his papers? heav'n what have I done? I'll instantly dispatch them after him Yet that were dang'rous too; they might miscarry; And then in person to return them to him, May cause another interview between us.— What mischiefs have I heap'd upon myself! [Goes off.]

SCENE V. Mr. ANDREWS's house. ANDREWS and JEFFER-SON. ANDREWS. What,—my old faithful steward!—O! impossible. And yet, this finding of the secret key Of the cash-chest, (with which he charg'd my wife) And medals in his trunk—but then the letter, Giving me information of this matter Has not the writer's name—that causes doubt— Then, his surprize, which seem'd so unaffected, With his most firm behaviour, so unlike The consciousness of guilt, when in his presence They were discover'd there, favour him much. Wherefore, till this affair be further canvass'd I wou'd not fend him to a public prison. [He walks to and fro.] JEFFER-SON. I shall obey.—He never judg'd more justly. [Aside, as he goes off.] Enter a Servant, with a letter to Mr. ANDREWS, which he reads. ANDREWS. The Speedwell cast away! a heavy loss! Ills upon Ills in train pursue each other. Heard you of this before? JEFFERSON. Such rumour was On the Exchange to-day, but not with certainty. ANDREWS. However she's insur'd, and highly too. Go fetch the policy, I wish to see it. Or rather wait me in the compting-house. JEFFER-SON. [As he goes off] O heav'n! I gave the money to his wife. [Exit.] ANDREWS. He seem'd confus'd, and mutter'd to himself; My fears anticipate some dread event. But what of this? shou'd it be heav'n's high will, That the remorseless billows should ingulf The remnant of my wealth; yet this—all this, I cou'd with patient resignation bear, And toil with pleasure for an honest pittance. But oh! to lose that precious, treasur'd gem, Which my whole soul engross'd—to see another, In my disgrace exult—yet more—yet more— My children—oh my children—must ye suffer! Away all thoughts of peace henceforth for ever. [Goes off.]

Scene VI. Lord WESTON's apartments. Lord BELMOUR and Lord WESTON. Lord BELMOUR. Well, nephew, have you yet consider'd better Of your love-frolick for the merchant's daughter? You may meet numbers through this spacious city With wealth superior far to her possessions; Nor need you languish for their hearts a moment. Lord WESTON. The common light shines not more unreserv'd; Their very charms fatigue the public eye. But, sir, my spirit scorns an easy conquest. Lord BELMOUR. Fine founding words, yet answer not my question. You too much from the world seclude yourself; Which serves to add fresh fuel to the flame. Long have I been, as I may say, your parent, And have at present in my thoughts for you, A wife well suited to your rank and fortune. Lord WESTON. Thanks, my good lord! I doubt not your kind wishes; But here, where all life's happiness depends, Permit me to determine for myself. True joys dwell only with united hearts, And solitude is far the wiser choice Than wedlock where domestic bliss is absent. How vain is then the hope of such delights With those of Fashion's stamp, whose only merit, Is, that they are of this all-conqu'ring sex,

Of ev'ry other excellence regardless? Lord BELMOUR.
Again, young lord, I tell you, shou'd you wed With the first
merchant's daughter of the world, 'Twould to your lineage be
disgrace for ever. Lord WESTON. Disgrace lies only in the
want of virtue, That excellence, in which she most abounds.
Lord BELMOUR. How long have you surrender'd to this
dotage? Lord WESTON. Almost from infancy; for even then,
A mutual sympathy inspir'd our souls; Which first com-
menc'd in her good father's house, (Whom I then serv'd,)
when all I knew of love, Was that her presence ever gave me
pleasure, As did her absence pain — I even thought, The air
blew sweeter from the place she breath'd. But when her
heav'nly mind disclos'd its beauties, My heart then fix'd beyond the power of change. Lord BELMOUR. All, all romance,
with which your head seems fill'd. But briefly to decide this
matter, know, 'Tis now full thirty summers since I wedded,
Yet have not had one offspring to inherit My large possessions, which I can bestow, As best my pleasure suits: and
you're the one, Who in my mind stands fairest for adoption;
My heir apparent, as my next a-kin. Reflect too, that your in-
come is unequal To that high rank in life, it shou'd support.
Lord WESTON. The more I lose, the more I prize myself, In
persevering thus — -but, my lov'd uncle! What can impede the
progress of my bliss, When your consent hath sanctified my
choice? Lord BELMOUR. What though I yielded once to your
fond suit, It is now rumour'd, and by all believ'd, Not only
that her father is reduc'd To bankruptcy and want, but that
the whole Of the large fortune which an uncle left her Is
wasted with the rest. Lord WESTON. Is this her fault? Is she
to suffer for another's act? Constantia hath that ever-during
worth, Which wealth or grandeur's glitter far outweighs:
That heav'nly mind, which will, when time hath cool'd The
fever of the heart, and reason rules, Cause mutual friendship
and domestic blessing. But shou'd ev'n this misfortune be as
rumour'd, I have this one occasion more of proving My constancy, and how I prize her virtues; Then, to secure for ever
that esteem By me preferr'd to all terrestrial blessings. Lord
BELMOUR. Infatuated boy! you form perfections Which only
have existence in your fancy. But pray, consider, what the

world will say. Lord WESTON. The world! base world! to censure gen'rous deeds; You mean, perhaps, my lord, those slaves of fashion, Who barter real for fictitious happiness; Alas! Their judgment is not worth a thought: If I'm approv'd of by the wife and honest, I shall be happy, and despise that world, Where virtue is discourag'd, — vice exalted, — Corruption an adopted cherish'd system, And ev'ry manly sentiment extinguish'd. Lord BELMOUR. For shame, young lord, call reason to your aid! Lord WESTON. From beauty only, it might have preserv'd me; But reason is Constantia's ceaseless advocate. Lord BELMOUR. Once more forsake her, if you prize my favour, The world's esteem, or your own future welfare. Away to distant regions; seek improvement; There is no love that absence cannot cure. Lord WESTON. Absence! — No death transcends that thought. — O sir! My fondness is to such excess, so true, That were heav'n's bliss assur'd me to forsake her, My soul might tremble for its own resolve. But what would worlds be worth with loss of honour! With loss of peace, its constant sure attendant! Lord BELMOUR. Since then all soothing arguments are fruitless; 'Tis fit t' apprize you that you yet remain Under my wardship by your father's will; And now to wed would be by law a nullity. Lord WESTON. Unrighteous, partial law! whose keen restraint 'Gainst female innocence alone is pointed, Whilst villains riot in its spoils unpunish'd; So that love's chaste, connubial joys no more, On its fleet wings, but in the tardy pace Of sordid interest move. But, thank kind heaven! My will is free to choose; else, my good lord, The parish proofs deceive. Lord BELMOUR. Perish all love! That one of the first families in Britain, Shou'd by such whims of folly be dishonour'd! A moment more, and I shall lose all patience! [He goes off hastily.] Lord WESTON. It grieves my soul that we should differ thus: He still has acted as a tender parent To me an orphan to his care intrusted. But pride and pageantry engross him wholly; With these, an avaricious selfish passion, For some years past hath quite possess'd his heart, And stagnated the streams of its benevolence, Save where by humour, or by pleasure prompted. But no mean views shall ever make me fight The sacred vows of love I once did plight. The heart

that's true, will still remain the same Though crosses press,
they but refine the flame And more sure joys the virtuous
passion wait With calm content, than with the pomp of state.
[Exit.]

ACT IV.

SCENE I. A room in Mr. GOODWIN's house. GOODWIN and WILSON. WILSON. This letter just now brought from our friend Andrews, Is superscrib'd to me, and yet most surely, By its contents, it was design'd for you. [Gives him the letter, which he reads.] GOODWIN. What proof this of his sad distracted state! Nor wonder; his distress encreases hourly. Midst which, one of his ships, it is reported, with a rich cargo, fraught from India's shores, Was lately wreek'd; and that by some neglect, It had not been insur'd. — 'Tis rumour'd too, That some of his acceptances are noted. WILSON. Most true, I have myself paid several; The just return to him, who, from his friends, His purse on like occasion ne'er with-held. GOODWIN. His bosom glows with all the heav'nly feelings Of gen'rous amity and social love. So boundless too, he cou'd not rest and know, That ev'n a worthy stranger felt distress. Enter a SERVANT and delivers a letter to Mr. Goodwin, which he opens and peruses. 'Tis all a mystery; or perfect madness. It can't be meant for me. [To the SERVANT.] Where got you this? SERVANT. Your neighbour Andrews sent it to your house. GOODWIN. Do you withdraw. [SERVANT withdraws.] I pray you hear it read. [Reads out.] "That you are the blackest of all villains you must yourself admit. What, induce me to suspect my wife with another (as you did this morning) in order to carry on your own adulterous schemes? such an attempt against my honour, peace of mind, and all that is most dear to me! If you regard your safety you will be cautious of our meeting. "James Andrews" WILSON. Give me the letter, 'twas design'd for me. Some like discourse as is in part there hinted, This morning pass'd between us — Give it, pray. GOODWIN. 'Tis plain, two misdirections have been written; Yet, let me stipulate this one condition, That you command yourself; for 'twill require Your utmost fortitude. [Gives the letter.] WILSON. By heav'n! some stratagem, Of deep and black contrivance is on foot; For there's no mischief, but that artful woman Hath heart and head to scheme. Enter a SERVANT. SERVANT. [To GOODWIN.] Sir, your friend

Andrews. GOODWIN. [To WILSON.] And do you choose to meet him? WILSON. Shou'd I shun him, It might induce him to conclude me guilty. GOODWIN. [To his SERVANT.] You—conduct him hither. I dread the event. [SERVANT goes off.] And yet well know your fortitude and temper. WILSON. Fear not.—I pity him; he's much disturb'd. Enter Mr. ANDREWS. ANDREWS. [To GOODWIN.] Did you receive some lines from me to-day? GOODWIN. To my surprize I did, which I suppose By the contents were otherwise intended. ANDREWS. Most strange mistake! I wrote them for that villain. WILSON. Ha! villain in my teeth, what mean you, sir? ANDREWS. Have you not wrong'd me? injur'd me most basely? WILSON. Unhappy man! 'twas never in my thoughts. ANDREWS. By heav'n, 'tis false! [To GOODWIN.] You have perus'd my letter. GOODWIN. I have by accident, as I inform'd you. ANDREWS. Is he not then the blackest of all villains? WILSON. Licentious railer, cease your foul invective, Nor patience press too far: but for that amity, In which we've liv'd, I cou'd not have endur'd Ev'n half of this unmerited ill-treatment. Again, I tell you, I'm an utter stranger To ev'ry charge in your impassion'd letter, Nor know I what it means. ANDREWS. Again, 'tis false. GOODWIN. O! my good friends, forbear; I've heard too much. Permit me then to speak between you both. What is affirm'd on one side, on the other As firmly is denied: wherefore, it lies On him who made the charge to shew his proof. ANDREWS. Then, at your instance only;—'twas a letter, From my ill-fated wife to this deceiver, Which on the way by accident I seiz'd; Wherein th' attempts he made (advantage taking Of the distress her indiscretion caus'd) To his adult'rous purpose to seduce her, Are manifest. WILSON. Deluded, undone man! How this insidious woman hath depriv'd him Of that sage judgment which he once possess'd! GOODWIN. Where is the letter? ANDREWS. Unluckily destroy'd. WILSON. And are these all the grounds on which you charge An old and faithful friend with such a breach Of virtue, honour, and of all that's worthy? O most abandon'd woman! weak as wicked. ANDREWS. Recal your words, base slanderer, else this hand Shall pluck forth the rude tongue that utter'd them. GOOD-

WIN. Forbear, I pray! you will alarm my family. WILSON. [To GOODWIN.] This is too much for ev'n a brother's bearing. Nor can I longer answer for myself. [Goes off.] ANDREWS. [After remaining for some time deep in thought.] Guilty! O guilty! every thing confirms it. Had my sworn enemy distress'd me thus, Time might have sooth'd the anguish of my soul; But oh! what mode of patience can endure To find the traitor in my bosom friend! GOODWIN. Rather think him innocent. ANDREWS. Yet how? Did not the blush of conscience mark his visage? The thought, the very thought, inflames to madness. GOODWIN. He seem'd surpriz'd, but shew'd no sign of guilt. 'Twere better sure, to sift this matter calmly; Passion but mars the purpose it pursues. ANDREWS. O! cou'd I hope for doubt! GOODWIN. You've known him long? ANDREWS. These thirty years; no brothers e'er lov'd better: And so exalted was, so pure the friendship, Which 'twixt our souls in harmony subsisted, Each knew no joy the other did not feel, And all our evils were by sharing lighten'd: He was my second self, as I was his, Like streams whose currents mix and flow together. GOODWIN. And have you ever found him in a falsehood? ANDREWS. In his fidelity I so confided, That with the dearest treasure of my soul I had entrusted him — and now he's lost; For ever lost — yet, yet to think — O heav'n! That this unhappy woman, once so virtuous, Cou'd ever thus have chang'd. O Goodwin! Goodwin! There's not a peasant in the clay-built hut, Who daily with his toil-tir'd arm acquires A scanty pittance for life's common wants, Whose state is not a paradise to mine! GOODWIN. Despond not thus, there's nothing certain yet; Wherefore, compose awhile your ruffled spirit, And bear with manly fortitude these trials: The tempest may th' inferior regions shake, Whilst those of higher sphere rest undisturb'd Above the threaten'd ruin! ANDREWS. [After some pause.] Oh! tell me then, what says report of her? GOODWIN. A dangerous request! ANDREWS. But cou'd you see your friend so deeply wrong'd? Wrong'd in the tenderest point! and yet be silent? What says the world of this lord Belmour's visits? You start — GOODWIN. Its rumours may be false — however, Since you so press it, I will thus far venture — Suppose, that after you have left the city, To sleep as usual at your rural dwelling, This, or some other night, you should return? And at some near-appointed station wait, Until some friendly watch, whom you can trust, Shall give you notice of the secret visit? ANDREWS. Thanks for this hint, it shall be so this night. GOODWIN. Mean while, you must be calm, or may prevent The purposes you covet to accomplish. [They go off.]

SCENE II. Mr. ANDREWS's house. Mrs. ANDREWS and MARIA. MARIA. Alas! what shall I do? 'tis I, 'tis I, That should be punish'd. Mrs. ANDREWS. Punish'd! for what? MARIA. I've brought my husband to a shameful end. Mrs. ANDREWS. Why this alarm? explain the mystery. MARIA. Your safety only, and a rash resentment (Not dreaming of the fatal consequence) Made me convey the key into his trunk. And Jefferson by note, without his signature, Inform'd your husband he shou'd find it there. Mrs. ANDREWS. Suspend, I pray you, your distress awhile. As yet, he's but imprison'd in his room: You know my husband has a tender heart, And loves him much. MARIA. Alas! his doom is fix'd: With everlasting infamy to wait On him, and his, how innocent soever; Nor shall I 'scape the bitter tongue of scandal. Mrs. AN-DREWS. Ere that shou'd happen, I'd accuse myself. Again then, I beseech you, be compos'd. And now, Maria, I've been just inform'd, That Jefferson withdrew some hours ago, And is not to be found. MARIA. And what of this? Mrs. AN-DREWS. Shou'd it be true, it must be thought by all, That the discovery of the secret key Was schem'd by him alone to screen himself. MARIA. You've quite reviv'd my spirits with the thought. I think the whole is like to fall on Jefferson. Mrs. ANDREWS. This night, I am to be at lady Meldmay's; But lady Belmour claims my first attention. MARIA. I thought that those unfortunate discoveries Had lower'd your spirits so, you had resolv'd To keep at home this night. Mrs. AN-DREWS. Your hit is just. But it is now too late to send excuse. Where's my husband? MARIA. He left the city, early. Mrs. ANDREWS. 'Tis time to dress — attend me at my toilet — — — [They go off.]

SCENE III. Mr. ANDREWS's house. LUCIA alone. LUCIA. I but now met him, and methought he shunn'd me. Unusual this from his most gentle nature. But deep distress seem'd on his brow imprinted, And rumours are unkind to him of late, Though none stood higher once in fair repute. O Jefferson! would I cou'd tear thee hence, From this fond heart, and its lost peace restore! — - But soft! I hear my dear Constantia's voice. Enter CONSTANTIA. CONSTANTIA. O Lucia! I'm of women most unhappy; No more must I of that chos'n youth have hope, In whom my ev'ry thought, my soul is center'd. LUCIA. You quite astonish me — it cannot be. Even the day was fix'd for your espousals. CONSTANTIA. O! but lord Belmour, his relentless uncle, Hath just now charg'd my father, that henceforth His visits here be countenanced no more; Vowing most solemnly, that shou'd we wed, He'd dis-inherit him. Besides in speech He hath much flighted us. LUCIA. Most distressful! CONSTANTIA. From such examples, Lucia, we may learn To dread those prospects of illusive fortune, Which shew like havens on a treach'rous shore, And lure us to our ruin. LUCIA. Happy man! How by the tyrant custom art thou favour'd! Canst speak the anguish of the love-sick heart, And from the hand that wounds implore relief: Whilst we in silent secrecy must shelter The deadly shaft, that rooted rankles there, And wastes the virgin bloom. Nor is this all; Should but the modest blush, the fault'ring speech, Or the disorder of the conscious soul, Betray the fondness it would fain conceal; Not only cold indifference, but neglect, Is full too oft the base return we meet. — CONSTANTIA. Ha! Lucia! whence these fears? am I despis'd? What have I done! I have betray'd myself. O! I conjure thee, by the sacred tie Of honour, friendship, confidence and love, Speak nought of this, but leave me to despair! LUCIA. Alas! 'tis my poor heart betrays itself. [Aside] Why to despair? by all those sacred ties! Thou wert not in my thoughts in what I've utter'd. Hath yet lord Weston heard these fatal tidings? CONSTANTIA. Full well you know how long he hath been absent: 'Tis that distracts my soul. — How hath he vow'd, That if a day pass'd by, and we asunder, He felt it as the absence of an age! LU-CIA. My dear Constantia! banish all such thoughts. He hath a soul superior to all falsehood. Affairs, 'tis said, of moment call'd him hence, And his return is ev'ry hour expected. CONSTANTIA. True, he is all that's gen'rous, great and noble, All that stirs envy and respect in man, Or love in woman. O my friend, my Lucia! Thou know'st not half the fondness of mine heart: Oft have I wish'd (so will love's fancy rave) That he had been the guardian of a flock, And I the sovereign of unbounded realms, To make him partner of that heart and throne: Or that we had been rear'd, 'midst rural innocence, A low, yet happy pair; with what delight, My tender frame had shared the harvest toil, To close with intercourse of souls the day! Enter a SERVANT. SERVANT. Madam, lord Weston's in the anti-chamber. CONSTANTIA. [To the SERVANT] Withdraw awhile— [He withdraws.] Be still, my flutt'ring heart! Haste, Lucia, if thou lov'st me, make excuse: Say, I am indispos'd—retir'd—yet stay. Why thus conceal the truth which must be known? Tell him, I cannot, must not, dare not see him— Yet, stay again—where is my father now? LUCIA. I know not; he went forth some hours ago. CONSTANTIA. 'Tis fit, lord Weston knows my father's orders, That I no more admit his visits here. Say, what would you advise? pause not, but speak. LUCIA. I'd see him, for the reason you have mention'd; Not rashly cast away a gem so precious. CONSTANTIA. How soon we yield to that the heart approves! Who waits without? [Enter a SERVANT] Conduct lord Weston hither. Enter Lord WESTON. LUCIA withdraws. Lord WESTON. Am I so bless'd to view thee once again! O! my Constantia, could'st thou but conceive What I have suffer'd in this tedious absence, Of which the cause hath been conceal'd from thee! Yet, whilst I languish'd on the verge of fate, Thy image ne'er forsook my tortur'd fancy, And its wild ravings were of nought but thee. CONSTANTIA. Would heav'n this interview had not been now! [Aside] Lord WESTON. Ha! not a word! not even a look this way! All ailments, every pang were ease to this. I read some dreadful sentence in thine eye.— What mean those shiverings?———Why that look of anguish? Sure, cruelty ne'er wore a form like thine! CONSTANTIA. What can I say? my tongue denies its office. [Aside] My lord, you have by this untimely visit, Led me to break my father's strict injunction. A father, dear as my heart's vital drops. Lord WESTON. What do I hear? O! are we not united? By sacred, mutual, faithful vows united? Of which I now am come to claim performance. CONSTANTIA. It is forbid—forbid, most sure, for ever! I'm but the daughter of a bankrupt citizen, (Th' ungentle terms with which I am reproach'd,) Of whom, shou'd you think more— Lord WESTON. What is't you mean? CONSTANTIA. Lord Belmour would renounce you then for ever; And 'tis most fit, my lord, you should comply. He is your uncle, and can much befriend you. Lord WESTON. O my Constantia! cruel, dear Constantia! Can'st thou conceive that any earthly views, Could for the loss of thee requite an heart, That cannot form a bliss from heav'n without thee? By that chaste passion, which no time can alter! Not mines of wealth, nor all life's splendid pomp, Can weigh with me against that worth of soul, With which thou art enrich'd so far above All others of thy sex I yet have seen, Far as thy beauteous form excels them all. Do but pronounce a peril, or a suffering To prove my constancy, save loss of thee. CONSTANTIA. My lord, these honours far exceed my merit. Lord WESTON. By heav'n! this coldness may to madness drive me. Am I to suffer for another's rashness, Of which, the new-born babe is not more innocent? Perhaps, some other hath usurp'd thine heart? 'Tis plain; too plain—You cannot doubt my truth! CONSTANTIA. Do not distress me thus—you know my heart; As well you know, that on that truth alone I would repose my ev'ry hope in life.— Lord WESTON. Then haste thee with me, and for ever bless me: A reverend priest attends to do the office, To which your father hath long since consented. CONSTANTIA. Oh! oh! forbear,—I shudder at the thought. I've told you all—You know a parent's right; Parent, not only of my life, but mind, Wherein he every wholesome seed implanted, And watch'd with never ceasing care their growth. Lord WESTON. Nor hath the soil been faithless to its trust. CONSTANTIA. Could you then hope from an unduteous daughter, To meet in wedded state, the due compliance Heav'n hath ordain'd, or I expect its blessings? You would yourself on serious thoughts condemn me. Lord WESTON. [He falls on his knees.] How far thou soar'st above all human excellence! And how thy virtues raise those peerless charms! I have transgress'd — -but Oh! vouchsafe thy pity! It was the zeal of fondness, and the fear Of losing thee, that urg'd me to the question, Which hath thy delicacy so offended. CONSTANTIA. O! if you ever lov'd me — prize my peace! Go, whilst my wav'ring heart can hold its purpose. These tell-tale eyes proclaim an interest there, Which time or fortune never can erase. But now this meeting might to both prove fatal. Lord WESTON. Wipe, wipe away that tear! thy sovereign pow'r Needs not an aid to bid my heart obey. Yet, O permit me, like the sentenc'd criminal, Who dreads the fatal stroke, awhile to parley! But go where e'er I may, my heart will bear The dear impression of thy image on it, Nor time nor absence ever shall efface it. [He goes off.] CONSTANTIA. How have I suffer'd by this forc'd behaviour, Gainst my soul's feelings, to this matchless youth! But O! in what enchanting, phrase, he urg'd His love, his fears and never-failing constancy! I cannot rest, till Lucia knows it all. [She goes off.]

SCENE IV. Lord BELMOUR's house. To Lady BELMOUR, enter a SERVANT. SERVANT. Mrs. Andrews waits upon your ladyship. Lady BELMOUR. Mrs. Andrews! — why did you admit her? SERVANT. I had conceiv'd it was your general order. Lady BELMOUR. I've chang'd my mind — I will not be at home; yet stay a little — tell her, I shall see her, At lady Meldmay's drawing-room to-night. [He goes off.] 'Tis like, she comes for what I got this morning: All which and more ill fortune swept away. Enter Mrs. ANDREWS. Mrs. ANDREWS. What! my good friend! my dearest lady Belmour! Not see her Andrews! her most faithful Andrews! 'Tis some mistake? perhaps, the servant's fault? Lady BELMOUR. He had my orders, though you thus intrude. Mrs. ANDREWS. Such a behaviour! — I am all amazement. — Whence is the cause? I pray explain yourself. Lady BELMOUR. If, madam, you are bent on altercation, I speedily shall leave you to yourself. So to your business, brief. — Mrs. ANDREWS. As you could wish; Then, the five hundred you this morning borrow'd. Lady BELMOUR. You surely dream, or are not in your senses! Mrs. ANDREWS. If I retain them long, 'tis not your fault. Lady Belmour! Honour! — Lady BELMOUR. Ha! this from you! When persons of my station condescend To such connexions, they most justly merit The treatment you have now presum'd to offer. Mrs. ANDREWS. You cannot surely mean to rob me thus? Lady BELMOUR. To rob you! you mistake; you owe me more Than will be ever in your pow'r to pay. Mrs. ANDREWS. For what I pray? Lady BELMOUR. You are not ignorant. Mrs. ANDREWS. I am, as I shall answer it to heaven. Lady BELMOUR. Not only for my husband's fond affection, But his fortune; which, (tis well known to all) He lavishes on you — so that your visits Can but reflect dishonour; wherefore, cease them. Mrs. ANDREWS. [Going off.] This is too much; ungrateful, faithless woman! [She goes off.] Lady BELMOUR. This treatment may hereafter serve her much. Even the meanest with the highest vie: Their manners as their fashions vainly aping, As might provoke the sourest spleen to laughter. [Exit.]

SCENE V. An inn on Cornhill near Mr. ANDREWS's house MARIA to the HOSTESS. MARIA. Madam, a ticket from this inn informs me, That some one in the house has wish'd to see me. HOSTESS. A person in a common peasant's habit, Came here some moments since and sent for you, Upon some pressing business, as he told me. MARIA. Is he here now? HOSTESS. He is; I'll shew the room. [They go off.]

SCENE VI. Changes to a back room. Lord BELMOUR in the habit of a countryman, and MARIA. Lord BELMOUR. Am I not well disguis'd? MARIA. Lord Belmour! — Wondrous! You might have pass'd me twenty times unknown. But pray, my lord, the purpose of this meeting? Lord BELMOUR. First say, how fares it with your lovely mistress? MARIA. Her present troubles are beyond expression. Oh! her distress is great. Lord BELMOUR. I'm on the rack. My fortune, life, my all's at her command. Unfold yourself, if you regard my peace. MARIA. Know then, her very ill success at play, (Which has of late ev'n all conception pass'd) Hath led her to use means, and such assistance, That she some honourable claims might answer, As otherwise she would have shudder'd at. And many a tale has reach'd her husband's ear. Lord BELMOUR. As I could wish. [Aside.] Unmerited ill fortune! MARIA. Oh! but this is not all. Lord BELMOUR. 'Tis, 'tis too much. Yet would I know the whole, that I may fly On expedition's wing to her relief.— Speak on.— MARIA. I cannot. Lord BEL-MOUR. Torture me no further. MARIA. Alas! my master cruelly hath charg'd her, (How shall I name it!) with indecent conduct; But chiefly, sir, with you. Lord BELMOUR. Most fortunate! This will outrun whole years of fond entreaty— [Aside] Ungen'rous, false accuser! thus to treat The loveliest of her sex; but first, Maria, We must relieve her from her present exigencies; With which somewhat acquainted, I, her friend, (None more sincere) am with the means prepar'd; And 'twas for that alone I schem'd this meeting. But for the purpose, you must so contrive it, As to convey me to her chamber secretly, This very night. MARIA. Heav'n! how you frighten me! I would not for the world do such an act. Lord BELMOUR. Your fears are without cause; I mean it only, Lest any prying babbler might observe us, At such late hour, as we must be together. And I can have none other opportunity, Of giving her the quick relief she needs. Wherefore, her friend must serve her at this juncture. I know your faithful heart.— MARIA. O! but my lord.— Lord BELMOUR. Behold these two, Maria; [Shews her two purses] each of these Contains an hundred pieces; one of them, You must vouchsafe at present to accept; The other, trust me, shall be also yours, Soon as I safely gain the wish'd-for station. [Puts one of the purses into her hand.] Your master left the city just at sunset? MARIA. My lord! my lord! Lord BELMOUR. You must, you shall accept it. MARIA. Well, my good lord, to save my in-jur'd mistress—[She puts up the purse in her pocket.] The backway thro' the warehouse is the safest, When the moon's down; for 'twill be late to-night, When she returns from lady Meldmay's supper. Lord BELMOUR. As sure as I exist—till then farewell! [He goes off.] MARIA. To what have I agreed?—Yet why repent? If not temptation proof, it matters not, When first she fails, or by whose means it happens; If she refills, I'll stand out to the last, And swear a thousand oaths, that I am innocent. At all events, there are two hundred pieces, Which will be most convenient, should my husband Be to a trial brought—So chance direct! [She goes off.]

ACT V.

SCENE I. An office in Mr. ANDREWS's house, and a CLERK sitting therein. Enter JEFFERSON in a cloak. JEFFERSON. Be not surpriz'd; it is an old acquaintance. Have a few moments absence so estrang'd you? CLERK. O Jefferson! those moments have occasion'd Many and various rumours of your fortune; Wherefore, permit me to rejoice to see you But whence this sudden ghastliness of visage The hue of death itself! JEFFERSON. It matters not. You never more may from this moment see me: — But this is foreign to me, present business. There are some matters of most deep concern Which I must straight impart to our good master; For which, this night I fought him at his villa, (Whither I heard he had resorted early) But much to my surprize, he was not there. I pray inform me, where I now may find him. CLERK. What shall I do? I am enjoin'd to secrecy. Are you full sure they're of such high concern As may excuse me in such breach of confidence? JEFFERSON. I should not else have urg'd it to you thus. CLERK. Try the new tavern in th' adjacent alley. (There, melancholy man, he waits my coming, At an approaching hour) [Aside.] But, Jefferson, Should you disclose who pointed out your course, I may for ever forfeit his regard. JEFFERSON. Rest well assur'd, no motive should compel it, And blessings wait upon thee for this kindness! CLERK. [To JEFFERSON as he goes off.] Yet hold awhile; I nearly had forgot. This night, the gentle Lucia fought you here, But disappointed, left you this remembrance. 'Tis for five hundred pounds. JEFFERSON. Too gen'rous maid! O! had my truant, and ungrateful heart Her merit justly priz'd, I might this day, In honour, as in virtue have been happy, Not thus a wretched outcast of the world — I pray return it with a thousand blessings — Heart-rending kindness! — Oh! — again farewell! [He goes off.] CLERK. His countenance betray'd some desp'rate fortune. Enter MARIA. MARIA. Was not that Jefferson? CLERK. 'Twas he indeed! MARIA. Undone! — undone for ever! — My poor husband! — [Aside] I spoke to him, but he declin'd an answer, And rush'd into the street.

CLERK. Unhappy youth! He told me I should ne'er behold him more. MARIA. Again I am at ease—[Aside.] But if for certain He hath our master plunder'd, as 'tis rumour'd, Should he not be secured? CLERK. His errand hither, Was to have seen our master. MARIA. Undone again! [Aside as she goes off.] CLERK. She seems not less disturb'd than him she fought. 'Tis fit I follow her, and seek her meanings, Which from her scatter'd words I could not gather. Besides, she mutter'd strangely to herself. Some sad disasters are I fear approaching, Whilst every countenance betrays distress. [He goes off.]

SCENE II. A room in a tavern. ANDREWS and JEFFERSON together, the first walking to and fro in much agitation. ANDREWS. And is this surely so? my blood runs chill. Oh! tell me, how, or when I've been thine enemy, That thou could'st calmly mean me all this mischief. I cannot credit it. JEFFERSON. 'Tis, 'tis too true— [Weeps.] ANDREWS. I once thought Jefferson the child of virtue. JEFFERSON. To fix me such, your lessons were not wanting. But oh! when we indulge one vicious passion, A train of others unforeseen will follow, Until at length all virtue is extinguish'd. ANDREWS. What's to be done! distress crowds on distress— — — Inhuman! barbarous! most abandon'd woman! And thou curs'd instrument!—Yet hold, my heart!— I see contrition in his mournful eye, And feel soft pity throbbing in my bosom: Deluded youth!—no object for revenge— [Aside] JEFFERSON. I am indeed accurs'd; I have betray'd The most indulgent master, best of friends! But you will shortly have sufficient vengeance. A dose I this night drank will rid me speedily Of that sad life I can endure no longer. ANDREWS. Oh! 'twas a desp'rate act!—Could'st thou conceive, A crime, to the Almighty so offensive, Would for thy other failings make atonement; May there not yet be help? JEFFERSON. 'Tis now too late, The deadly drug, works far, and I grow faint— ANDREWS. 'Twere better to have liv'd whole years in penitence, Or wild despair, to expiate your guilt. JEFFERSON. Oh! cou'd I hope for your assisting prayers, 'Twou'd be some comfort to my fainting soul. You are so good, you cannot but

have interest In those blest dwellings, whence my foul of-
fences May have excluded me, alas, for ever! Nor dare I lift or
eye or hand for mercy. ANDREWS. Sad-fated youth! my own
distracted state Is suited ill to intercourse with heaven. But
lose no time yourself: that righteous judge, Whom you have
so repeatedly offended, Abounds in mercy, as he doth in justice; And pray'r is at his throne a pow'rful advocate. JEFFER-
SON. And you, as sure as that Great Pow'r is just, Will meet
the due reward of all your virtues. When I go hence, I pray
you read this paper— My fate draws near—-so now, farewel
for ever! [He goes off.] ANDREWS. What horrid images
crowd on my soul! Yet worse may follow—blood perchance
and murder— But will not injur'd honour,—ruin'd peace, For
ever ruin'd, justify revenge!— [Pauses.] I am resolv'd—So for
this writing now— [He opens it and reads.] "Most injured Sir,
Inclos'd you have my will by which, as some small recompense for the many wrongs I have done you, I have be-
queathed you all the little fortune I have left. Oh! lend your
prayers, and pity a repentant wretched sinner. William Jefferson." Some recompense!—There can be none for me. The
moment is at hand, the fearful moment, When I'm to seek for
that, which, when discover'd, My sure perdition seals—yet
even certainty Were ease to that I feel—tremendous state! Like some benighted traveller quite 'wilder'd, I see no friendly
ray to guide my steps— But 'midst my woes, I've let this hap-
less youth, Plung'd in despair, escape me unattended. I'll haste to seek him out—Yet, cannot now: Troubles more intimate
claim ev'ry thought. Enter one of his CLERKS. I near despair'd of seeing you: 'tis almost light. What has delay'd you
so? CLERK. It was your wife. ANDREWS. My wife! CLERK.
Yes, sir, she's but at home some moments. ANDREWS. Was
she attended? CLERK. One went in before her. ANDREWS.
What, into my house? CLERK. Yes, sir. ANDREWS. Man, or
woman? CLERK. A man, sir. ANDREWS. Hah!—And know
you who he is? CLERK. Lord Belmour, sir. ANDREWS. Are
you sure? CLERK. As I exist— For waiting, as 'twas your de-
sire I should, 'Till I could warn you of your wife's return,
And walking 'twixt the dwelling and the warehouse, I by a
light, which glimmer'd from the moon, Then almost waned,

descry'd a man and woman Close standing at the wicket of the gate, That leads into the lane. I stood conceal'd, Until lord Belmour and Maria pass'd me Towards the house. ANDREWS. Can I now pass that way? CLERK. You may; I lock'd the doors, and have the keys. ANDREWS. Come, deep and sweet revenge! 'twere virtue here. [Aside] It must be near the dawn. Go on, I'll follow. Life's now a curse; death then my only wish.

SCENE III. Mr. ANDREWS's house. THOMAS and MARIA. MARIA. Who releas'd you? THOMAS. Our unhappy master. MARIA. Is he in town, and up at this late hour? THOMAS. He's in the house; and heaven grant, Maria, He holds his reason: for he rush'd impetuous, With looks as madness wild, into the room, Where I sat tied; when falling on his knees, He crav'd my pardon; then, from my bruis'd arms He cut the cords, and hastily ran off. MARIA. Which way? THOMAS. Towards the compting-house. MARIA. O heav'n! THOMAS. Why this alarm? MARIA. His arms are there. THOMAS. 'Tis true, And never man appear'd more desperate. Wherefore, as ev'n a moment's loss were dangerous; I'll for his neighbours speed, Wilson and Goodwin. [He goes off.] MARIA. The mischief is at hand, and 'twill require My deepest skill, or I'm undone for ever. But to the last I will assert my innocence. [A bell rings.] This is my mistress, and from her bedchamber. [Rings again.] Again it rings; and with unusual violence. — I must away — What fights may meet me now! — [She goes off.]

SCENE IV. Another apartment. CONSTANTIA and LUCIA. CONSTANTIA. Oh! Lucia, Lucia, I shall die with terrours — What can these noises mean? [A groan is heard.] Heard you that groan? LUCIA. Sure life expir'd with it! — A woman's voice — Enter hastily WILSON and GOODWIN, THOMAS and other Servants, at which CONSTANTIA and LUCIA shriek. CONSTANTIA. Protect us, heaven! — what are you? WILSON. A messenger, In utmost hurry rous'd us from our beds, And pray'd us to haste hither with all speed, To save a family. CONSTANTIA. Oh sirs! — heav'n grant 'Tis not too late — some sad event, I dread — [A groan, and then another]

They're from the room where Mrs. Andrews sleeps.
[CONSTANTIA swoons, and is taken of with LUCIA.] Enter
MARIA. MARIA. Woe! woe unutterable!—fights of horrour!
All welt'ring in their gore—haste! haste with me. [They go
off.] [Back Scene opens and discovers Mrs. ANDREWS's bedchamber— Lord BELMOUR on the ground with his sword in
his hand bloody, and Mr. ANDREWS with his also drawn
and bloody, in a fix'd posture, resting on it, and looking on
the ground.] GOODWIN. O heav'n! what havock's here! [To
ANDREWS] Alas! my friend, What have you done? WIL-
SON. He's quite insensible. Perhaps this woman can inform
us—speak— MARIA. I will, I will. Hearing the bell twice
rung With violence unusual from the chamber In which my
mistress lay, I thither flew; Where entering, with amazement
I beheld Lord Belmour there, and her upon her knees: Sudden, my master, with an unsheath'd sword In rage rush'd in,
and instantly assail'd him, (Who also had drawn his) they
fought awhile; When with a hideous groan lord Belmour
reel'd, Bit quick recovering, with doubled fury At his
assailant made—when, she, quite wild, Rush'd on lord Belmour's sword, and fell with him. WILSON. 'Tis better done
by him, than by our friend. ANDREWS. Done—What done?
all is not done as yet—this— [He is going to stab himself,
GOODWIN and WILSON rush on him, and wrest his sword
from him.] GOODWIN. What would your madness do? too
much already, This fatal scene exhibits to our view.
ANDREWS. Deaf, deaf to all,—away,—away with counsel!—
'Tis clear as noonday light—burst—burst, my brain!— Lord
BELMOUR. Listen—oh listen to a dying criminal— Your
wife is innocent—I, I alone— ANDREWS. Peace, villain,
peace!—how came you in her chamber? Lord BELMOUR.
Without her knowledge—Oh! 'twas by that woman, [Poin-
ting to MARIA] My vile accomplice in the soul attempt. MA-
RIA. Mercy! O mercy! and I'll tell the whole. Oh! she is innocent—I, all to blame— WILSON. 'Tis fit a magistrate be sent
for instantly; As also meet assistance to these wounded, Who
seem to need it much. [A servant goes off.] Lord BELMOUR.
Good sirs! Let me be hence convey'd—I can't escape— And
heav'n will in some moments give full justice. [He is led out.]

ANDREWS. And let me also fly these scenes of horrour, Or I shall wilder be than the chain'd wretch That beats the dungeon walls. [As he is passing by Mrs. ANDREWS, she seizes the skirt of his coat.] Mrs. ANDREWS. Oh sir!—my husband!— ANDREWS. Take! take the vile adultress from my sight. Mrs. ANDREWS. For charity, forbear those bitter words. True, I have injur'd you beyond all hopes Either of your indulgence, or heav'n's mercy. But by that Pow'r! before whose just tribunal, I shortly shall be summon'd to appear, My soul abhors the base imputed guilt, (How strong soe'er appearance speak against me) Ev'n in thought. ANDREWS. Abandon'd, faithless woman! Oh! that her foul disgrace clos'd with her eyes! Then might I undisturb'd behold this havock. [Aside] Did not I, find you on your knees to him? Mrs. ANDREWS. I was beseeching him to leave the room. ANDREWS. How came he there? Mrs. ANDREWS. By the same Pow'r supreme! You're not yourself of that event more ignorant. Soon as my woman for the night had left me, He from the closet rush'd into my chamber. ANDREWS. Oh! I have been too hasty—much too rash. — — — Mrs. ANDREWS. You will not think so, when you hear the whole. The wretched nobleman, you now have punish'd, Is not less guilty than if I had yielded. Yet, think not that I mean t' acquit myself; My conduct led him to the vile attempt: And, oh! with rage and thirst of vengeance fir'd, I was too busy in th' infernal plot, Contain'd in that false letter to your friend, The honest, gen'rous, and most faithful Wilson. I also had your old and trusty steward Accus'd of crimes to which he was a stranger; And Jefferson to me owes his perdition. ANDREWS. Cease! cease! pour self-convicting mourner, cease! — This cannot be — 'tis the sick fancy's dream. Mrs. ANDREWS. Oh! that it were untrue, as thou art kind. Yes; this, all this, and more I have committed. I have undone thee—I, thy bosom's favourite,— And am the fatal source of all these horrors. But my swift hast'ning fate will be some recompence. — I bleed within apace, and grow most faint — — — How happy was I once, and how ungrateful! ANDREWS. 'Tis, 'tis too much— Mrs. ANDREWS. Alas! I see it is. — How these reflections rack my madding brain!— Turn, Oh! turn that tender aspect from me! 'Tis worse than scorpion rods, or

whips of steel. Abhor me; scorn me; tear me from thy fondness, And every imprecation pour upon me: For hope is fled,
and I would court despair. Some suff'rings here might lessen
those hereafter, I would not covet else a moment's life. —
ANDREWS. Would I could sooth her tortur'd soul to rest!
Her sorrows rend my heart. — Oh thou sweet penitent!
There's not an angel in the heav'nly mansions, That will not
sue for thee. Mrs. ANDREWS. Yet, there is something I
would petition as my last request — Let me conjure thee then,
most injur'd excellence! By all the happy hours we liv'd together, Ere one infernal passion seiz'd my heart! Have pity on
the harmless, dear-lov'd innocents, Whom I must leave
amidst a cruel world! And when you shall my rueful story
tell, Be thus far kind, and say, as is the truth, Oh! say, she was
not an adultress. ANDREWS. I will, I'll speak thee as my soul
conceives thee, Spotless, and free as Virtue's self from ble-
mish. Mrs. ANDREWS. Then, may with me, thy sorrows have an end! — ANDREWS. Oh! canst thou then forgive my
wild upbraiding? Mrs. ANDREWS. I blame thee not — so let
me be convey'd From thy dread presence, and this fatal spot:
They are too much for weakness to endure. ANDREWS. No,
no, I'll watch thee whilst a single spark Of that lov'd life
remains, and sooth thy woes. Mrs. ANDREWS. Too kind! —
Forbear! — Were your fond wish indulg'd, It would but add
new weight to your afflictions. Oh! agonizing thoughts! — Oh!
my pour soul! — ANDREWS. She droops; she dies — and oh!
by saving me — Physicians, surgeons, ev'ry help be sent
for! — Mrs. ANDREWS. 'Twere fruitless all unless their
friendly aid Some balm could minister to deep despair — Rage on, distress — -haste, madness! quench my soul — Hark!
hark! that voice! — — — the door of mercy's clos'd —
ANDREWS. [To the attendants.] Straightaway, convey her
hence to mine own chamber. [She is carried off, and as he is
following her, several bailiffs enter rudely with CONSTAN-
TIA.] CONSTANTIA. Protect my father, heav'n! undone —
undone — WILSON. What can these ruffians mean? whom
do you seek? Bailiff. He is our prisoner on several writs.
[Pointing to Mr. ANDREWS] ANDREWS. Ay, ay, come on —
'Tis fit I shou'd be punish'd. Take, drag me hence, ye minis-

ters of justice! Death, death, or madness only can relieve me. GOODWIN. What is the whole demand? Bailiff. Above four thousand? WILSON. He shall not sink for that: I'll be his pledge. ANDREWS. Most gen'rous, injur'd friend, this is too much. GOODWIN. [To WILSON.] I'll join you in the bonds. — Prepare them, sirs. [To the bailiffs, who go off] CONSTANTIA. Thanks, best of friends! but you shall never suffer. My fortune, independent of my father, Far more than this for which you have engag'd, Shall be our pledg'd securi- ty. ANDREWS. Daggers! — — — daggers! Wasted — all wasted, in the general wreck. [Aside] WILSON. 'Tis fit lord Weston should be straight appriz'd Of the sad fate of his unhappy uncle; These two nights past, since his return to town, He hath repos'd with me. GOODWIN. I hear his voice. Enter lord WESTON hastily. Lord WESTON. Where, where's my father! take, O take your son! And let me fly as such into y- our arms! Just hearing of your undeserv'd calamities, From your remorseless creditors below, I have engag'd for all their claim'd demands, And come to wipe the tear from ev'ry eye. ANDREWS. Cold sweats bedew my feeble, trembling limbs, And ev'ry object round me grows a blank. Good heav'n! sup- port me, to these tasks unequal — — — [As he is falling, WIL- SON and THOMAS support him.] WILSON. The feelings of his heart o'erpow'r him so, He cannot give them vent; it may prove fatal — — — He's all convuls'd: let's place him on this seat. [CONSTANTIA attends him.] Lord WESTON. [He mo- ves towards CONSTANTIA.] My angel — My Constantia! O those tears! And looks of desperation pierce my soul. Your father lives — Fortune again may favour: But I am your's, and will be so for ever. WILSON. O my good lord! There are di- sasters yet within these walls, More fatal far, which claim our instant aid. Lord WESTON. I've heard them all — my uncle is no more — Would that he had not fall'n in such a cause! WIL- SON. But heav'n hath will'd it, and we must submit. With smiles delusive, other crimes decoy, To hazard future ills for present joy: Gaming alone no transient rapture knows, No gleam of pleasure for eternal woes; Distrust and anxious fears its birth attend; And wild distraction waits its guilty end.